MW01194446

THE
CYRUS
MANDATE

A JACK GARRISON NOVEL

Ray
BENTLEY

Bodie
THOENE

Research by Brock Thoene

MARANATHA
PRESS

PRAISE FOR THE ELIJAH CHRONICLES

"Ray Bentley is one of my favorite people in the world, let alone a world class pastor, author, and prophecy expert. Refreshing is his ability to combine more than just deep interest and scholarship with his countless Holy Land trips, but also a deep devotion to the truth of the Word. And teaming with the Thoenes—Middle East experts in their own right—makes it even better."

—JERRY B. JENKINS,
New York Times
Best Selling Author

"...Bodie Thoene expertly weaves an intriguing plot through current events, while Ray Bentley adds a depth of understanding to complicated Middle East issues. The combination is a gripping story that has meaning..."

—ANNE GRAHAM LOTZ,
Author and Speaker

"The biblical insight of Ray Bentley and the storytelling flair of Bodie Thoene have produced a timely and thrilling novel..."

—DINESH D'SOUZA,
**Bestselling Author
and Film Maker**

THE CYRUS MANDATE

A JACK GARRISON NOVEL

THE ELIJAH CHRONICLES
Book 3

THE CYRUS MANDATE

Cataloging-in-publication data on file with the Library of Congress

Cover Design by Tyler Novak and Zach Andrews for raybentley.com

Interior Design by Lamp Post Publishers | www.lamppostpubs.com

Produced by www.raybentley.com

ISBN: 979-8-6869-7246-9

Printed in the United States

Published by

MARANATHA
PRESS

10752 Coastwood Road
San Diego, CA 92127

Dedicated to my Dad, Rayburn John Bentley, Sr.

The first of our family to see the light,
and the Father and Patriarch of our tribe.

PROLOGUE

"And I stood upon the sand of the sea,
and saw a beast rise up out of the sea...."
Revelation 13:1 (KJV)

December 26, 2019

The dark, cloudless sky and the dull, predawn waters of the Persian Gulf, blended into borderless pewter.

It was Christmas holiday. Twelve scholars from King's College, London, gathered barefoot on the beach at the city of Al Wakrah in Qatar.

They had fled the winter gloom of England and traveled south on holiday for the last annular eclipse of the decade. Students, cameras in hand, whispered in small groups. Warm, gentle waves lapped the shoreline as they waited for sunrise.

Los Angeles Times journalist, Tabitha Vanderhorst, twenty-nine years old, tall, blond and attractive, was the only

American among the Brits. She hugged her knees, closed her eyes, inhaled the sea air, and dug her toes into the fine white sand. A hot cup of coffee and a Krispy Kreme donut would make her life perfect about now.

"So, California girl, what do you think of the beaches in Qatar?" Ryan Henry passed her coffee in a paper cup. His curly, ginger-colored hair was a tangled mop, making him seem much younger than his years. "No donuts. Sorry."

Tabitha shrugged and patted the sand, inviting Ryan to sit beside her. "Very different than home."

"How so?"

"Central coast shores are craggy, beautiful. Untamed." She inhaled the strong aroma of the steaming brew. "Not like here. Seems so peaceful here."

"Peaceful is hardly the word for the Persian Gulf."

"You're talking politics again."

"And you're talking like a woman trying to escape politics."

"I need a break, for sure."

"Okay, then. So how is the Persian Gulf different than your home?"

"At home the ocean is, you know, a sort of dark green. Waves always crashing on the shore. When I walk on the beach at home I feel something…."

"Untamed?"

"Wild, sort of. Like British beaches in Cornwall. I like your English coast. Familiar."

"I'm glad." He leaned closer and kissed her shoulder. "And Qatar?"

"Oil wells. Skyscrapers. Sand." She raised her cup to her lips. "Good coffee though."

Ryan frowned. "Not exciting? I beg to differ. The hub of all history. Past and future. Directly across the gulf is Iran. Ancient Persia. Two thousand years ago we would have stood right here and watched the galley fleets of great conquerors sail past. Yes. Iran. Just there—where the sun will rise. And Turkey is that direction. To the far north is Russia. That direction is Saudi Arabia. And, of course, Israel."

She resisted the urge to laugh. Ryan knew everything, it seemed. Ryan, with his professorial British accent, was too eager to impress her with just how much he knew. It was working. She was impressed.

She leaned in and whispered, "Ryan, you just named most of the players in Armageddon."

He paused, pondering. "Oh. Right. If you believe that sort of thing. I suppose. Past and future. Yes."

Majoring in political science, Ryan had traveled to the Middle East several times with his father who was some sort of Royal in the House of Lords, as well as a senior executive with British Petroleum.

Ryan had convinced Tabitha to escape the bone-chilling cold of London and spend a few weeks traveling through the Middle East, writing stories for the *Los Angeles Times* and working on an archeological site in Israel before she was to return to Los Angeles.

"Well, anyway." He glanced at his Rolex and handed her protective glasses. "In about seven minutes, together we shall witness the last annular eclipse of the decade at its rising. In a full eclipse the corona of the sun shines like a bright engagement ring from behind the shadow of the moon. This is an annular eclipse. Partial eclipse. Momentous, however. Something we will tell our children about one day."

Tabitha stiffened and stared out at the flat surface of the sea. Did he mean "our" children, she wondered? Children they would have together? Was this a sort of proposal? She felt his gaze on her.

"Well?" he asked. "What do you say?"

She laughed nervously. "I don't even know what an annular eclipse is."

"Let me tell you, then. You see, the sun will rise there… in the east. The moon is between the earth and the sun. That's the eclipse part of the equation. An annular eclipse means that the moon is further away from earth than usual so the disk looks smaller as it covers the sun. We probably won't see the sun's true corona, but a ring of fire, a corona, if you will, seems to radiate from the sun, and just for a moment, as the moon moves away, a bright beam will radiate outward—like the diamond on an engagement ring. Clear?"

Tabitha was silent for a moment, still not sure where Ryan was heading with this. "Oh," she replied. "Sure."

"Good. And then we'll spend a few weeks in Israel. You'll meet my old mentor."

"Jerusalem. I'm looking forward to seeing Jerusalem."

Tabitha knew Ryan was more interested in being with her than he was in seeing the eclipse. For the last year he had been pursuing her. At first Tabitha thought it was hopeless, but he was always finding ways to make her smile. Starbucks coffee on a beach in Qatar, for example. She could not resist. His nerdy thoughtfulness had finally left her hopelessly in love.

She noticed the bulge in his shirt pocket. The shape of a ring box? Tabitha resisted the urge to stare at it. "Yes," she said. "A great adventure. Thanks, Ryan. Glad you convinced me to come along. I would have been sitting alone in my freezing little flat." She raised her cup in a toast. "So. Merry Christmas."

"Happy Christmas."

He gazed deeply into her eyes, then turned away. Fixing his sights on an oil tanker moving slowly across the grey water he muttered, "The face that launched a thousand ships. A girl like you should never be alone."

Tabitha quickly changed the subject. "I hope the tanker won't block our view."

Ryan nodded and raised his enormous camera to peer through the viewfinder. "Russian tanker. It's all about oil, you know." Pausing, he pointed east. "We'll see the eclipse on the horizon just there. You ready?"

Someone shouted, "Two minutes! Get ready!"

A hush settled over the group. Cameras and protective eye gear in place, the students stood and gazed expectantly toward an intense red glow just beginning to light the distance. There was land across the water. Low headlands and scattered islands emerged from the darkness.

It was not what Tabitha expected of a sunrise. A flat, black disk obscured the distant shore. The moon was a blot on the horizon.

"Where's the sun?" Tabitha asked. "The ring?"

"Shhh," someone urged, as if the solar event was an intensely spiritual revelation.

One sharp prong of crimson burst from the sea.

"Ahh...." the crowd sighed.

Moments later, another glowing red horn of fire erupted from the water.

"It's mid-eclipse," Ryan explained tersely. "But the moon's not completely over the sun. It's partially blocking the center of the sun. See there."

Instinctively, Tabitha raised one hand to silence him.

Creeping skyward, on either side of the moon's shadow, the sun's two crimson horns grew in size and intensity; ominous spikes piercing the air above Iran.

A middle-aged man among the crowd of observers muttered nervously as he snapped a photo, "I'll title this one, 'The Beast Rising from the Sea.'"

A few in the group laughed uncomfortably at the stranger's attempted humor.

Ryan peered intently through his lens, snapping one photo after another.

The partially-eclipsed sun emerged. It was neither

golden, nor a ring, nor even circular; a corona of malevolent flares.

Instead, somehow, the angry, fiery glow remained rooted
on the Persian Gulf, while the horns—sharply defined in
crimson and amber—were silhouetted against the grey
heavens crowning a monstrous head.

Someone gasped in alarm.

Belatedly, Tabitha recognized she had uttered the
cry herself.

No one seemed able to speak or move. All were transfixed at the sight of the rising beast. It seemed to Tabitha
like something out of a science-fiction movie.

At length the bottom of the moon rose above the water,
revealing the sun's shape to be a thin crescent. It was, she
thought, much like the flag of Islam.

A thin, unpleasantly warm wind rose with the sun, tossing sand in Tabitha's face. Was there a quavering howl on
the wind?

"Did you hear that?" she whispered. "An evil sound."

Ryan shook his head and pressed his lips together.
"Nothing," he replied. "I heard—nothing."

At last the Russian tanker slid between the sun and
the shore.

Turning abruptly toward Ryan, Tabitha caught his
motion as he thrust something back into his shirt pocket.
"So much for my romantic moment." At her questioning
look he inclined his head and gestured for her to follow. "I
think we're done here."

_____   ✧ ✧ ✧   _____

It was a cold Jerusalem night, January 27, 2020. A dusting of snow fell over the city. Jack opened the curtains of his bedroom to watch just before he fell into a deep sleep. He was aware of the presence of his old friend Eliyahu before he opened his eyes. Eliyahiu—the Old Testament Prophet Elijah—had appeared to Jack in many dreams and visions; guiding Jack's journey from disbelief to fully committed Jewish believer in Yeshua and staunch supporter of Israel.

"Come with me," Eliyahu commanded.

"What is it?" Jack asked, getting up and following the prophet.

"Something has happened on this day. On this very day. You must see and mark the date."

Jack and Eliyahu walked along the parapet of the wall overlooking the Old City.

Prime Minister Benjamin Netanyahu was in Washington, D.C. with President Trump, discussing what the President called "The Deal of the Century."

"This is God's own beloved land," Eliyahu said, looking out as the first streetlights lit the night. His gaze seemed to see the ancient past and the future. "You must understand, my son, that what is about to unfold upon the world begins with this terrible risk. President Trump believes that no matter what is proposed, the Palestinians will reject it. He has another way, but the Enemy will fight against it."

Jack nodded in agreement. "It has been clear from the start that Israel's application of sovereignty over Judea and Samaria could only happen with the agreement of the United States."

"And today that approval has been delayed," Eliyahu explained, though the news had not yet broken. "Netanyahu would have annexed the biblical lands of Israel long ago. But now the proposal for division of the land has been put forth. The plan calls for Israel to annex a portion of the West Bank, and calls for the creation of a disarmed Palestinian state. The enemies of Israel will not accept this, but even so, remember this date. A great upheaval is coming upon the world today."

"Today? Now?"

"Look." Eliyahu waved his hand toward the west, giving Jack a global view of the world. Something like a sickly green fog swirled across China. It was swept on the wind towards the shores of America. "The prophet Amos predicted this day. This very day." From the wall, Eliyahu lifted his chin and cupped his hands around his mouth to shout the prophecy of Amos.

"Woe to you who are complacent in Zion, and you who feel secure on Mount Samaria, you notable men of the foremost nation, to whom the people of Israel come!"

Jack knew that there was only one foremost nation whom Israel looked to for help and advice. America! The

image of the United Nations in New York suddenly reared
up before Jack. The great buildings and shadowed steel
canyons of New York City shimmered in a vision.

Eliyahu continued, "You put off the evil day and bring
near a reign of terror. You lie on beds inlaid with ivory,
and lounge on your couches. You dine on choice lambs
and fattened calves. But you do not grieve over the ruin
of Joseph!"

Jack knew well that the lands of the West Bank had been
apportioned by God as the territories of the sons of Joseph.

Eliyahu shouted louder. "Your feasting and lounging
will end! The Sovereign Lord has sworn by Himself—the
Lord God Almighty declares: I will deliver up the city and
everything in it."

As Jack watched, the date, January 27, 2020, flashed
across the giant news screens in Times Square.

"Today!" Jack cried.

Tendrils of contagion rose up and reached out from the
heart of China. From the beaks of vultures sickness was
vomited down over New York City and surged through
the streets.

From China to New York, the great American city
was the first to be touched by it. Buildings were boarded
up. Sickness rolled through the streets and into houses. It
swirled around the United Nations, surrounding the building like a stinking green swamp.

Eliyahu raised his hands and cried, "If ten men are left
in the house, they too will die. And if a relative who is to

burn the bodies comes to carry them out of the house and asks if anyone is still hiding there, 'Is anyone with you?' and he says, 'No,' then he will say, 'Hush! We must not mention the name of the Lord.'

For the Lord has given the command,

And He will smash the great house into pieces

And the small house into bits."

As if in a film, Jack saw the crumbling of the World Trade Center on 9-11, and then the skyscrapers of New York lit up in celebration of abortion. The buildings were tipped with red, like the blood of syringes!

The prophecy had been coming true for many years.

And now! Today! Before Jack's eyes, the hospitals of New York City overflowed with sick. Body bags were packed into refrigerator trucks parked in the parking lots of medical buildings.

The fog of plague continued to flow out from New York, spreading to all the capitals of the world and to the great cities of America.

Jack cried, "Can't this be stopped? Have mercy, Lord!"

Eliyahu's eyes brimmed with tears as he turned to Jack. "This plague is not the will of the Almighty. He longs for the hearts of all to repent and be turned to Himself. He is not willing that any should perish, but that all would turn to His Son, Yeshua, for forgiveness and salvation."

Jack fell to his knees and wept. "This must not be. Have mercy, Lord! Forgive!"

Eliyahu replied, "Pray the Lord will relent."

At this, Jack saw the Lord standing by a wall that had been built true to plumb. He was holding a plumb line in His hand.

He did not speak, but Jack knew the meaning of the vision. Things which had been built true and straight must be set true again.

Eliyahu lifted Jack to his feet. "The hearts of His people must return, or there will be many more judgments to come. Look to the past and you will know what the future is meant to be. Go: study and learn all you can."

1

ISRAEL AND AMERICA

Jack Garrison had first met David Levin when Jack had
been recruited by the Israeli Office of Public Diplomacy
and Media. Since that initial conference, Jack had accompanied visiting pastors from the U.S. and other countries on
tours around Israel. Given Jack's professional resume—he
had been a fact-finder for the London-based European
Committee on Mid-East Policy—he was well-versed in the
rhetoric of anti-Israeli sentiment. Now, as a whole-hearted
supporter of the Jewish state, as well as a student of prophecy, Jack Garrison was the ideal representative to correct
modern misunderstandings, accidental or deliberate.

Jack repulsed Hamas and Hezbollah anti-Israel propaganda with well-reasoned discussions, and personal anec-
dotes about Palestinian terrorist attacks—one of which had

almost cost Bette Deekmann—now Jack's fiancé—her life. None of the guide duties since had been as dangerous—but some had been every bit as argumentative. Anti-Semitism was alive and well in the modern world, and Jack loved engaging with—and was successful in confronting—the Boycott-Divest-Sanction crowd.

So successful had Jack been in educating American pastors from politically-biased denominations that he was much in demand by the Israeli government. He was not surprised when David Levin asked for another meeting.

"So, David," Jack said cheerfully as the two shook hands. "What do you have for me this time?"

There were more lines on Levin's face than when they'd first met, Jack thought, but the smile that stretched from boyish chin to round spectacles was as genuine as ever. "Sit down, Jack," Levin offered. "Tea?"

"I'm good, thanks."

"So first my news: I've been promoted."

"Mazel tov," Jack offered. "So I'm here to meet your replacement?"

"No," Levin replied slowly. "I really want to have you continue working with me—but let me explain."

Jack was intrigued. David Levin was always a straight shooter and a straight speaker. Middle Eastern conversations often had an element of mystery about motive and agenda, but Jack had never experienced it with Levin.

Levin resumed. "My promotion is really more of a lateral move. My boss—the Head of Public Diplomacy—has his office right next to the Director of Political Affairs. They seem to think I have something to offer in both areas, so I'm now Assistant Director of Public Diplomacy and Political Affairs."

"Twice as much work, but not twice as much pay?" Jack quipped.

"Something like that. Jack," Levin said intensely, leaning forward. "What do you know about current Israeli-Arab relations?"

"Is this like an oral defense of my doctoral dissertation?"

When Levin did not respond, Jack dropped the attempted humor. "Okay, here I go: Saudi Arabia and the United Arab Emirates are more scared of Iran and Iran's nuclear capability than they ever were of Israel. Iran is Shia Muslim and Persian; not Arab or Sunni Muslim. The Arab Persian Gulf states rightly fear that Iran wants their oil. Behind the scenes, the House of Ibn Saud, and Egypt, and other moderate Arab nations are cooperating with Israel, in security and economic issues, better than ever before. How am I doing?"

"So far, spot on. Got any proof?"

Jack nodded. "Bibi's visit to Oman. New synagogues in Arab countries like Dubai and Abu Dhabi. Arab regional sporting events that now invite Israeli athletes—something unthinkable ten years ago."

"Five years ago," Levin corrected. "Thanks to social media, a hundred thousand Arabs tune in daily to learn about Israel and Judaism, and to get the world news their own repressive governments forbid them to have. But what hurdles are there opposing this kumbaya moment?"

"Arabia cannot be too public in supporting Israel or face rebellion in their kingdom," Jack noted. "Iran funds terrorist organizations and promotes anti-Israel sentiment and tries to subvert Arabia. Russia is still a player, bending unrest in Syria and Iraq for its own purposes. Turkey is more Islamist than ever. The U.S. is more aligned with Israel than any time since Harry Truman, but is also walking a political tightrope because of BDS and pro-Palestinian propaganda on college campuses. Enough?"

"Almost," Levin corrected. "What other player on the world stage is there?"

Jack thought it over. "China," he said finally. "Where's China in all this?"

"Exactly," Levin agreed. "We...." The plural pronoun hung in the air for a moment. "We have reason to believe that something is coming out of China for which the propaganda machines will try to blame Israel."

"Come out of China—like what, for instance?"

Levin shook his head. "Not clear yet. Tons of rumors. Big, but not necessarily military. Perhaps more in the nature of an economic attack. China wants to supplant the U.S. as the economic powerhouse in the world. Whatever targets the U.S. ultimately also targets Israel, yes?"

"Cyber-attack?" Jack guessed.

Levin shrugged. "I'm not in the spy business, Jack. But when something is revealed, I need to have someone reliable to speak to America about it; counter the lies, as it were. I may need to ask you to return to the U.S. on a moment's notice."

"And you think what's coming is that urgent?"

"You wouldn't be here and I wouldn't be asking if I didn't think so."

"All right," Jack replied. "I'm in. Two stipulations, first."

Levin nodded for Jack to proceed.

"One," Jack said. "Bette and I are getting married. We are honeymooning in Paris. No cell phones. No emails. She doesn't know anything about that yet—it's a surprise. If you interrupt our time in Paris it better be life-or-death."

"Got it," Levin agreed. "And the other point?"

"Whatever you ask me to do is for me alone. Bette is no longer in the security service and she's not my bodyguard. Clear?"

"Of course," Levin said, rising to again shake Jack's hand. "And—thank you."

✡ ✡ ✡

History books, facsimiles of ancient maps, and copies of documents were spread across Jack's desk in a disorganized order that only he could decipher.

Bette and her younger brother Benjamin eyed him skeptically from across the heap of chaos. "It's research, Benni," Bette teased. "You get used to the scramble after awhile."

Jack teased in turn. "Don't listen to your sister. I promised you true tales of buried treasure, and that's what we have here."

Benjamin leaned in expectantly. "Alright, then. Let's have it."

Jack read aloud the story of Jeremiah and the Temple treasures from Second Maccabees, chapter two. "This record recounts it was Jeremiah the prophet who commanded those who went into captivity to hide some of the fire of the altar. He also ordered them not to forget the commandments of the Lord and warned them not to be deceived in their thinking when they saw the gold and silver idols with their ornaments. With similar speeches he told them to keep the Law of Moses in their hearts." Jack paused and took a swig of water before continuing with the passage.

"The same records tell us how God told the prophet to take the Tabernacle and the Ark with him until he came to the mountain where Moses had looked out over the land God had promised to give His people. When Jeremiah arrived there, he found an empty cave into which he carried the Tabernacle, the Ark, and the altar of incense. Then he blocked the entrance. Some who followed him wanted to mark the place, but they could not find it. When Jeremiah heard this, he rebuked them, saying, 'This place will be hidden until God gathers His people together again and shows them His mercy. Then the Lord will reveal these things, and the glory of the Lord will appear in a cloud, as in the days of Moses and again when Solomon prayed that the Temple might be specially set apart for God.'"

Bette fixed her gaze on Benjamin. "You have questions, Benni?"

The boy frowned. "Where do I start?"

Jack raised his chin slightly as he considered Benjamin's earnest expression. "What's the first thing that came into your mind?"

Benjamin leaned close and tapped the passage in Maccabees. "Here, for instance. What records show this? Where is it written anywhere but here that Jeremiah hid the Ark in a cave in Mount Pisgah?"

Jack shook his head, "Only here, Second Maccabees 2. Makes a great movie plot, eh?"

Benjamin remarked, "It's been done."

Bette said to Benjamin, "I think we should call you Indiana Jones."

"Right," Jack picked up the account from verse thirteen. "These same things were written in the records and in the memoirs of Nehemiah. It is recorded that Nehemiah established a library by collecting the books about the kings and the prophets, the writings of David, and the letters of the kings concerning offerings to fulfill vows. Likewise, Judah collected all the books that were lost in our war, and now they are in our possession. If you need these things, send someone to get them for you."

A thoughtful silence fell over the room as Jack finished reading. As the trio contemplated the information,

Benjamin asked quietly, "An ancient library full of documents? History and letters of kings? But where is it now?"

Jack closed the book. "Some say this is all legend. Others believe the library was destroyed in AD 70 when the Romans sacked Jerusalem and tore down the Second Temple."

"But what do *you* believe?" Bette asked. "Is it the Dead Sea Scrolls?"

"Maybe. Almost all the of the writings of the Prophet Isaiah were there—essential foretelling of the miraculous rebirth of Israel. And then there is the famous Copper Scroll, also found at Qumran. One of the most famous artifacts in history! Of over nine hundred Dead Sea scrolls, it's the only one written on metal! It lists places where various treasures—gold, silver, precious things—are buried. Things that go back to Solomon's Temple. Maybe even to the Tabernacle of Moses! The most commonly used words in the scroll are 'dig,' 'cubits,' and 'gold.'"

Benni seized the excitement. "So what have they dug up? Where is it?"

Shaking his head, Jack replied, "None of the treasures described in it have been found—yet. No one had been allowed to carry out a thorough investigation. It is in the Jordan Valley, and hung up by politics."

To counteract Benni's obvious disappointment, Jack added, "But listen to this: the layout of the Qumran settlement is a detailed model of Jerusalem; like a detailed, three dimensional map. So maybe all that treasure? Maybe it's all right here, under our very feet."

All three students of prophecy involuntarily glanced downward, then grinned at each other.

When the excitement subsided a little, Jack continued, "I do believe there is also another ancient library yet to be revealed. I have heard the library still exists, mostly intact, hidden deep beneath the Temple Mount. There are some who say they actually knew men who had been in the tunnels and had seen it."

"And the Ark of the Covenant?" Benjamin's expression seemed much older than his years. "The Tabernacle?"

"Apparently not ever restored to the Second Temple."

Conversation stopped. All three remained lost in visions of secret cave entrances, golden vessels, ancient clay tablets, and hidden marvels.

✧ ✧ ✧

When Bette and Benni went home, it was almost midnight, but Jack's research was not yet done. The streets of Jerusalem were empty. Jack stood alone before the Great Seal of the United States carved on the stone of the American Embassy in Jerusalem. What was he supposed to learn about how ancient prophecy connected to a modern nation like America that had not even existed when the prophecy was delivered?

He carefully studied the symbols of the seal, aware that everything pictured carried great significance, but he was unsure of all the meanings.

Just beneath the image of the seal was the name of the president who had brought the American Embassy to Jerusalem, and proclaimed the City to be the undivided capital of Israel.

Donald J. Trump

President

The date of dedication was May 14, 2018; the seventy year anniversary of Israel's Declaration of Statehood.

Jack felt the presence of Eliyahu on his right hand before he saw him.

"Shalom, Jack," Eliyahu said, as though greeting an old friend on passing in the street.

"Shalom." Jack kept his gaze on the seal.

"What are you doing here?" Eliyahu stepped closer.

"I think you know better than I do." Jack glanced at the prophet, who was dressed in a modern, white, open collar shirt and dark trousers like any ordinary Israeli. "Tell me what I am supposed to be looking for?"

Eliyahu's brown eyes sparkled with amusement. "Haven't you learned?"

"Yes. Everything means something. Yes. Yes. I know. But what in this am I supposed to see?"

"What is the date?"

"May 14, 2018."

"Dedicated seventy years to the day since the rebirth of Israel as a nation. Seventy years since May 14, 1948. One of the most significant numbers in all of scripture."

"And America's president moves our Embassy...."

"There's much more to it than that. We will see it all. All of it. Everything. Thirteen is the number repeated over and over again on the seal. Starting at the top. You see? Thirteen stars."

"For the number of the thirteen original states."

"Oh, but in the promises of the Almighty, the stars mean so much more!" With a wave of Eliyahu's hand, a scroll appeared before Jack upon which were written in letters of fire the covenant promise between God and Abraham. "Read it," Eliyahu instructed.

"The Lord took him outside and said, 'Look up at the heavens and count the stars—if indeed you can count them.' Then He said to him, 'So shall your offspring be.' Abram believed the Lord, and He credited it to him as righteousness."

Jack frowned as the scroll flared up and vanished.

Eliyahu waited a long moment before he again spoke. "There are twelve tribes of Israel. And the thirteenth star is Yeshua, Jesus, the promised King and Savior of Israel. In Him, all the nations of the world are blessed. The story of mankind's salvation is pictured in thirteen constellations in the stars. As the Lord promised Abraham, his descendants are like the stars, so numerous they cannot be counted. Listen closely and understand." Eliyahu captured Jack in his somber gaze.

"The number thirteen is throughout America's symbols. Thirteen colonies, right? I want to understand," Jack replied.

"Do you not know the thirteen attributes of God's Mercy?"

Again Eliyahu waved his hand and another scroll with burning letters appeared. "Read."

The words, marked with different biblical references, were intertwined like filigreed gold. Jack nodded, speaking carefully. "'The Lord, the Lord, a God merciful and gracious, full of compassion, plenteous in mercy and truth, slow to anger, and abounding in steadfast love and faithfulness, keeping steadfast love for thousands, forgiving iniquity and transgression and sin, great in power.'"

Eliyahu seemed pleased. "So you see: Thirteen are the attributes of the Almighty. Thirteen is the number of America; all nations of the world are gathered there, and blessed through this nation." He pointed at the motto on the ribbon in the eagle's beak. "Read!" he commanded.

"E Pluribus Unum. Out of many, One."

Once again glowing letters flared. "Read!" Eliyahu ordered.

"But those who wait upon the Lord shall renew their strength; they shall mount up with wings as eagles, they shall run and not be weary, they shall walk and not faint. Keep silence before Me, O coastlands, and let the people renew their strength! Let them come near, then let them speak!"

Jack scanned the passage again. "The eagle."

"Yes." Eliyahu agreed. "Now look at what the American Eagle holds in his talons."

Jack leaned closer. "Thirteen arrows in one bundle; a symbol of American strength. An olive branch, symbol of peace, in the other." Jack paused. "This seems important. Very important. What is it I am not seeing here?"

Eliyahu gratified by the question. "Look," he gestured to the seal of Israel. "The olive tree is also part of the emblem of Israel: a menorah surrounded by olive branches. And the connection is plain in Scripture. It is written: Israel is the great olive tree. The roots go deep into the promises of HaShem. And America? E Pluribus Unum—the Christian gentile nation of America—like the true church—is the wild olive branch of scripture, grafted into the olive tree of Israel. Your Founding Fathers, inspired by the Ruach ha Kodesh, though they did not see the holy vision clearly, spoke forth the promises of Romans 11. The union of America with Israel is engraved in stone even here in Jerusalem on the Great Seal of America."

Jack's eyes widened. "So…America is truly linked to Israel."

"Now count the olive leaves upon the Great Seal. And count the olives."

Jack dutifully obeyed. "Thirteen olive leaves and thirteen olives."

"So. As America holds tightly to the Word of God it will hold tightly to Israel. Tell me Jack, what have you learned about the biblical number thirteen and America's Great Seal?"

"Thirteen is the number representing the qualities of

God's mercy," Jack repeated, finally understanding how closely America's blessings were linked to Israel.

"America. From its very beginning it was the last refuge for persecuted Jews. America was the refuge and a safe gathering place for Jews who would one day return to the land of Israel. The first Jews who settled on the American continent believed that they would be safe there until the End of Days when Messiah called them to return to their homeland. And it was the same for persecuted gentile believers. America was the refuge from the religious tyranny of kings. The American nation was established for all who seek to worship the One True God of Israel, and for those who kneel to no other king but Jesus, the King of Heaven! Three American presidents, like King Cyrus of old, confirmed America's covenant blessings are rooted in the bond with Israel. The first president to proclaim the refuge was George Washington. Then Harry Truman; May 14, 1948. And now Trump; May 14, 2018. Thus it is written in this stone."

"Everything means something," Jack whispered in awe. The lesson was at an end. Jack reached up to touch the great seal on America's Jerusalem Embassy.

When he turned again, Eliyahu was gone.

✧ ✧ ✧

"America in prophecy?" Dr. Adam Scheer, Professor of World Religion at Harvard, leaned back in his chair and eyed the Zoom-transmitted image of Lev with disdain. He brushed away the idea of America in Scripture as though it was a buzzing fly.

Lev's brown eyes crinkled at the corners with amusement at the man's arrogance. "You teach world religion and yet you are unaware of biblical prophecy concerning Israel and America?"

"You must be joking," Scheer scoffed. "Not even Evangelical End Time fanatics can find America in their lists of Bible verses."

Knowing Lev well enough to read his thoughts on the matter, Jack half smiled and waited for Lev's response.

"It's there. Significantly. Historically."

The professor fired off another round. "I keep up with the so-called Evangelical prophets. The most common teaching is that it's quite possible that the United States as we know it will be destroyed in the last days. It has nothing to do with the survival of Israel, one way or the other, or some metaphorical Rule of Christ."

Lev unsheathed his pocket Bible and opened it to the book of Revelation, chapter three. Without prior explanation he began to read aloud. "To the angel in the church of Philadelphia write: These are the words of Him who is holy and true, who holds the key of David. What He opens no one can shut, and what He shuts no one can open. I know your deeds. See, I have placed before you an open door that no one can shut. I know you have little strength, yet you have kept My word and have not denied my name."

Dr. Scheer, visibly offended despite being several thousand miles distant, sat erect, challenging Lev; challenging the Scripture. "You can't believe that reference literally applies to America," he smirked. "Or that anything in Revelation can be taken at face value?"

Lev raised his brows. "Oh? So your statement of faith is that the Scriptures of the end times cannot be taken literally?"

"Who believes this any more? For two thousand years people have been saying a physical Jesus was returning. He hasn't returned. He won't return in that way. America is not found in the Bible. There will be no America because the Second Coming is a metaphor for a One World Government. A world of unity under one political Leader. If America stands in the way, it will be destroyed."

With a slight shrug, Lev continued reading from Revelation 3. "Since you have kept My commandment to endure patiently, I will also keep you from the hour of trial that is going to come upon the whole world to test those who live upon the earth. I am coming soon. Hold on to what you have so that no one will take your crown. Him who overcomes I will make a pillar in the temple of my God."

"Of course there will be difficult times," Scheer argued, "erasing borders and creating a world where all nations are united. Our current American president is the greatest example of the turmoil caused by isolationism. Make America Great Again? This Republican President and his vision of America has been the greatest impediment to our vision of global unity. The nations of Israel and America together are the road block to world peace."

Leaning into the frame from its margin Jack interjected, "Our Founders were men fleeing oppression. In 1630, eleven ships arrived in Massachusetts Bay. They were filled with persecuted Puritans and religious dissenters. Their escape to the New World was literally an act of desperation. A matter of life or death. In their Great Charter, John Winthrop, leader of the company said, 'We shall be as a City on a Hill; The eyes of all people are upon us.' Since then America has been the beacon of freedom. That original Charter is the founding document of the American Constitution. Based on biblical principles, men are created equal and endowed by their Creator with inalienable rights: life, liberty and the pursuit of happiness. From the earliest days America was a refuge for people of all religions. Jews, in particular, had never had religious freedom until they arrived on American shores."

Dr. Scheer scoffed, "Winthrop's great experiment didn't work very well, did it?"

"The American Republic has worked better than any government which has ever existed," Lev argued.

"Better? Look around you. A season of turmoil would bring America to its knees. And it would not be getting up again."

Jack asked the instructor, "You are an American citizen, and yet you believe that?"

The professor retorted, "Sure. I carry an American

passport. It's temporary. I consider myself a citizen of the world. As I look into the future I see one world religion. One humanity. Every man, woman, and child will all soon be injected with a microchip which will hold all our personal information, including a global passport as identification. One government will exist, where, for thousands of years, mankind has squabbled over borders and territory. And that is my interpretation of the book of Revelation and the metaphor of Christ coming to earth."

Lev continued, "I believe America is the Revelation 3 church of Philadelphia."

Scheer erupted in a loud derisive laugh. "Philadelphia? It was an ancient city in Asia Minor!"

"Ancient Philadelphia was destroyed by an earthquake in the second century," Lev continued. "The Philadelphia passage in Revelation 3 is speaking of the end of the age and a small, but faithful church. Unlike the other six churches, Philadelphia remains faithful through horrific apostasy until the Second Coming. I believe this passage speaks directly to the foundational American church."

Jack picked up the thread. "Philadelphia was the place the Declaration of Independence was written and proclaimed in 1776. Philadelphia was the first capital of the new nation. The Constitutional Congress met in Philadelphia. Our Constitution, guaranteeing religious freedom, was created in Philadelphia."

Lev continued, "And in recent history—May 14, 1948 —America's immediate recognition and support of the re-establishment of Israel makes the biblical connection even more absolute."

Again the professor guffawed. "Now I've heard everything. This is the first time anyone has suggested such a ludicrous link between America and Israel. And to suggest that the Revelation 3 church of Philadelphia is a prophecy about the preservation of America? Come now! Not even your own band of right wing religious fanatics would believe this theory."

Lev folded his hands across his chest and smiled. His face expressed the old adage about casting pearls before swine.

Jack clicked "End Meeting," a moment after Dr. Scheer had stabbed "Leave meeting." The discussion with the Harvard professor had come to its predictable conclusion.

✧ ✧ ✧

American newspaper correspondent, Tabitha Vanderhorst, rang the bell at the gate of Jack's grandmother, Dodi. Tabitha's upturned, masked face spoke into the security camera when Jack answered.

"Shalom." She held her journalism ID up to the lens. "I'm Tabitha Vanderhorst. Here for the pre-interview. To meet the artist...."

Jack buzzed her in through the gate, watching the screen until the lock clicked behind her and she crossed the courtyard.

Jack escorted her in as Bette prepared refreshments. Dodi, her head tilted to listen to their approaching footsteps, was seated in her favorite over-stuffed chair in her studio. Straight-backed, elegant, and composed, she extended her hand when the writer approached.

It was, Jack thought, almost like an audience with a royal. Dodi's original art, displayed on easels and mounted on the walls, surrounded her.

Tabitha Vanderhorst , in awe of Dodi's art as she greeted the legendary artist, did not notice that Dodi was blind.

"I have wanted to meet you for so many years." Tabitha took a seat across from Dodi. Jack and Bette joined the circle.

"I'm so pleased to meet you, young lady," Dodi remarked.

Jack noted that Dodi called the visitor young, though her features were hidden. Dodi was seeing with her heart, he surmised, just as she did when she captured an image on canvas.

Tabitha removed her note pad. "I couldn't believe it when the Israeli media department actually said you would see me. I'm in Israel mostly for political pieces. Only time for a few stories which really interest me."

"And I am one of those rare pieces? A true Israeli antiquity," Dodi laughed.

Tabitha glanced at Bette uncomfortably as if to ask if she had offended the great artist. Bette gave her a nod of encouragement.

"Your art has been a part of my growing up, you see. Your story."

Jack interjected, "My grandmother doesn't tell her personal story often. Never on film. What you're asking would be very unusual."

"I know that. Some small details are available on Wikipedia. Fragments of your story. That's all I could glean. But I think maybe America needs a fresh look at what it means to survive the Holocaust and then go on to create something of such beauty. Your lifetime is a body of work. All beautiful and full of ethereal light though there is such darkness in the events of your past. You are awe-inspiring, really."

Bette poured Dodi's tea, then placed the cup in her hand. This was the first hint Tabitha had that Israel's great Artist of Light could no longer visually distinguish light from darkness.

Tabitha faltered a moment, gazing at Dodi questioningly.

"You were saying, dear?" Dodi asked.

"I would like to ask if I might film your story. Interview you. Write a piece for publication in the *L.A. Times*, but also for film and for social media posting. For posterity?"

Dodi inhaled deeply and said to Jack. "Jack? What do you think? Is it time for such a thing?"

Jack nodded. "I can't think of anything more important if you're up for it."

"Well, then," Dodi deeply inhaled the fragrance of her tea. "I will answer you in this way: one can watch a person sip a cup of tea on a screen, but one cannot taste the flavor.

Nor can one smell the aroma. Nor feel the steam on one's face." She paused. "Do you understand my meaning?"

"I think so," Tabitha replied. "But please. Help me understand."

"I have never allowed my story to be told on camera. Because though it is a true story, the listener or viewer will never be able to truly feel the grief I felt giving up my child to save her life. No one can taste the salt of my tears, or experience what I felt trying to swallow a morsel of food because sorrow nearly choked me. No one can imagine our bodies packed in the cattle cars, pulling from the rail station. Or hear the cries of loved ones parting when some went to the left and others to the right. Who can understand what it is to be a Jew? To survive when so many others perish? Who can know what it means to come here to Israel; to a Jewish homeland?"

"I understand," Tabitha looked downward. "I do understand."

Dodi continued, "You see, my dear, I can see it all vividly even now. Experience it. I can hear it. Smell the smoke. Taste the ash in the air. Feel the grit beneath my fingers at will. But how can I share those things? If I had spent my life remembering those things, what kind of life would I have lived? How will speaking of those things now convey the reality?"

The room was silent except for the trickle of the water fountain outside in the courtyard.

At last Dodi continued. "So I decided. I asked God

how I could help. Ah, color and light. These things made
by God give hope: a single dandelion growing through the
crack in the courtyard of the concentration camp. That
was a miracle. It was a wonder of delight in the midst of
gray death and black despair. And so, I have not wanted
to speak of the sorrow and the hopelessness that was then.
The depths of that evil are unfathomable. I wanted instead
to paint for the hearts of the broken; lifted, when they catch
sight of that single dandelion."

Jack glanced at Bette, whose eyes reflected the grief
of her own loss; a family slaughtered by terrorists. Bette
looked up and kept her gaze steadily on Dodi's painting
called, "Dandelion at the Western Wall."

Dodi asked, "What shall I do, Jack? If I speak of these
things will I not destroy all the hope my art has given
the world?"

Jack considered the question. "Perhaps if you can say
what you have just said. The dandelion. Maybe?"

Dodi addressed Tabitha, "My dear, have you visited
Yad Vashem? Have you been to the Holocaust Museum in
Washington, D.C.? Have you seen the piles of abandoned
luggage? Or the room of shoes?"

Tabitha shook her head in solemn admission.
She had not.

Jack replied for her, knowing that Dodi could not see the
response. "She hasn't."

Dodi lifted her chin slightly. "You must. Those empty
shoes are the reason Israel must exist. If you wish to film

my story—me telling my story—you must go. Look at the names carved there, and know my name might have been there among them. I was among them. One of them. There are names written there who are people I know. Knew. I remember their smiles and our conversations. I remember sitting at a café table in Paris and discussing Hitler plotting in far away Berlin. And then Hitler was there. In Paris."

"Alright," Tabitha agreed to the terms. "I will go."

Dodi replied, "Alright. When you have been, then I will speak."

✡ ✡ ✡

Brahim Rahman paced up and down the polished marble floor. He pounded his right fist into his left palm as he expressed his frustration. "It should never have happened," he protested. "By now Israel should be the pariah of the world! I had the Europeans all in my hands; the American churches and the American universities with their support of Boycott-Divest-Sanction—it was all so perfectly planned."

Rahman's voice rose a half tone in pitch as his frustration grew. "Now even some Muslims have fallen out with each other! Some are for making peace with Israel! And I—I—barely escaped arrest and prosecution in England. It cost an enormous amount of money and surrendered favors to resolve. What's to be done?"

The question was addressed to the only other occupant of the Budapest office of the Open Society Alliance. The lined face with the sagging jowls betrayed disapproval and a faint smirk at Rahman's lack of control.

"Calm yourself, Brahim," instructed the chairman of the OSA. "Your hatred of Israel is commendable, but your focus is too narrow. You must realize that America and Israel must and will fall together. Already things are in motion to topple America's global economic leadership. Six months or a year of shuttered businesses, and soaring unemployment, and inflationary government spending and U.S. support of Israel will falter. Then we will have approached the threshold of a One World Government—wherein a hero will be needed to return order from chaos. All that is required is another crisis or two to push the younger generation of Americans into our way of thinking."

"You have such an event planned?" Rahman asked eagerly.

The man whose name in his native Hungarian meant 'next in line,' but whose adopted surname in Greek meant Bone Box, scoffed at his visitor. "Have you learned nothing? Once the major device is at work—as I assure you it is—the next crisis requires no manufacturing. Something suitable will present itself. It always does. Almost an entire generation of bright, young Americans have been trained by their colleges that the USA is—what do our Iranian friends say? The Great Satan. Israel is only the Little Satan.

"So when the next social upheaval arises, white, affluent college students will flock to the banner of overturning the "American fascist regime." Down with America! Down with Israel! You see? The two are inevitably linked."

Rahman stopped pacing and settled into the embrace of a leather armchair across the desk from his mentor. "I know you're correct," he proclaimed. "I know the time is near for a new world leader to step onto the stage." Rahman's words were not entirely sincere. He did not expect the aging mastermind to survive into his ambition of global leadership. Nevertheless, a little flattery was in order when addressing the greatest opponent of democracy and capitalism—and Israel—in the world. "I know that I have failed you," he said. "How can I regain your trust?"

"Ask yourself that question," Bone Box urged. "Is there no obstacle that must be removed?"

It was an almost audible voice that whispered in Rahman's ear; so clear and so intense was the advice that he nodded his agreement. "Yes, of course. The nexus of what has thwarted me in the U.K. and in Israel is one man—Jack Garrison."

The impossibly rich man with the dual Hungarian and American citizenship steepled his fingers together and smiled. "A good place to start, don't you think?" Hunching his shoulders and leaning forward he warned: "So. Garrison must not be allowed to interfere with my plans for the United States. Agreed?"

"Agreed. He and that troublesome Deekmann Jewish woman are getting married."

"And you will keep track of them?"

"Or perhaps more than just that."

"See to it," Bone Box ordered.

2

NEVER FORGET

Cool, morning sunlight glistened on the Rechelim Winery. Broad green leaves rustled around heavy clusters of purple grapes; soon ripe for harvest.

"There are one hundred eighty acres of vines," Jack Garrison explained to his grandmother Dodi, who leaned heavily against his arm.

Jack could spot the different varieties of grapes by the various shades of green on the hillside: Cabernet, Shiraz, Merlot, and Viognier.

The aroma of new wine wafted from the huge fermentation vats in the buildings at the bottom of the hill.

Lon Silver, silent financial partner in Rechelim, waved his unlit cigar toward a grove of oaks at the top of the hill and leaned in to address Dodi. "So? What do you think,

Dodi? Do you approve? A good place for your grandson's wedding?"

The old woman raised her chin slightly and inhaled
deeply. "It is exquisite." She smiled and from behind her
sunglasses she pretended she could see every detail, every
color, of the scene. "A vineyard, named for the three Rachels.
The first Rachel, beloved of Jacob, and two Rachels who died
in our day as martyrs for Israel. I could not have imagined a
more beautiful place for Jack and Bette's wedding."

Dodi, an artist whose paintings were considered
a national treasure in Israel, was slowly going blind.
Glaucoma was stealing the vision of this woman whose
entire world had revolved around a palette of color
and light.

Even so, Jack pretended all was well with his grandmother. He and Bette agreed to give his Dodi the honor of
choosing the perfect setting for their wedding.

The exact location of the ceremony would be a surprise
for Bette.

"So what do you think?" Jack asked. "Will
Bette like it?"

Dodi pressed her cheek against Jack's arm. "If I had
my brushes and my paints here I would capture it for you
children on canvas forever. Oh, Jack, I loved Rechelim
Vineyard the first time I ever laid eyes on it. So much like
the vineyards in France where your grandfather and I so
loved to go before the Nazis overran our home."

"Well, then?" Lon's deep, earthy voice inquired. "So?

It is settled?" He extended his hand to Dodi as if to clasp hands in a bargain. She did not see it.

"Indeed," Dodi agreed. "This may be the wedding of my grandson, but I promise it will be the happiest day of my life."

"Let's go back to the house and seal the deal with a cup of tea and biscuits?" Lon led the way slowly back to the Land Rover.

Dodi laughed, "Tea and biscuits when we're at one of Israel's best wineries? Lon! Don't you have a glass of your finest wine and a plate of cheese for us to share on such a momentous day?"

Dodi clung tightly to Jack's arm as Lon guided them into the cool, dark, barrel room of the winery. Racks of oak casks loomed like a canyon above a long olivewood table, with seating for at least two dozen diners.

Jack was certain that Dodi could not see in the dim light. He guided her to a chair at the head of the table, and sat down close to her. He remained silent as the two pioneers shared their hearts.

Dodi ran her aged fingers over the smooth wood and smiled. "It's beautiful," she said. "Olive?"

Lon lit a candle and set it in front of her. "An ancient olive tree. Massive. It was cut down by terrorists the year we planted the first vines. A statement by our enemies that the tree of Israel would not survive. I was a young man and it grieved me. I thought how much it had survived, centuries, only to be destroyed by haters of Israel."

Dodi kept her cloudy eyes fixed on the candle flame.

"And out of the destruction someone created a holy table. And here it is. Fit for celebrations of life."

Lon was pleased by her observation. "You know what sharing food and wine means to a Jew. Weddings. Bar Mitzvahs. Circumcisions. My family celebrates Seder here every year. So many important occasions in our lives."

Dodi grasped the thick edge of the ancient tree. "Your artistry?" she asked.

Lon selected a bottle of wine. "Yes. My work. Two years. And when I finished, I knew everything this fallen tree had to tell me about our people and our land."

"They bury us, not knowing we are seeds."

"And when I finished, and the table was set up here in the barrel room, I was no longer grieved. No longer angry. I knew what it meant."

Lon poured the wine into three shining goblets engraved with an olive tree. Jack guided Dodi's hand to the stem. She raised her cup and waited while Lon and Jack tapped their glasses upon hers in a toast.

Dodi whispered with a voice filled with emotion. "And here we are, like the old olive tree. So we toast things to come! To the wedding of my grandson Jack and my soon-to-be granddaughter Bette. To life! L'Chaim!"

✿ ✿ ✿

On the other side of the Kidron Valley sprawled the city of Jerusalem. The westering sun recast the prominent Muslim shrine from a golden dome into an onyx silhouette outlined in orange. In Jack's eyes the structure resembled a hulking beast, crouching atop the Temple Mount.

From Jack's vantage point on the Mount of Olives he looked down across acres of headstones—Jewish graves. Over one hundred thousand tombs, from all eras of Jewish history, supplanted previous centuries of olive groves. Like barren trees surviving a wintry blast, those buried there confidently expected to spring to life again. Each longed to be among the first to welcome the coming of Messiah.

With that imagery in his thoughts, Jack was not at all surprised when the modern sights in front of him flickered and disappeared. The Old City of Jerusalem reappeared as he had seen it in visions of the eras before the Roman destruction in AD 70.

Just a little below the brow of the hill were a group of men. Bearded, dressed in muted brown or pale beige robes, they clustered about their leader, whose back was to Jack.

Eliyahu stood beside Jack's right shoulder. "Do you know when we are?" he inquired.

Jack nodded. "I can guess," he said. "That's Yeshua and his disciples. Let me listen."

"Rabbi," began a thin man whose worn sandals and deeply lined face reflected years of tramping in the sun and sleeping outdoors, "You have said that the Temple of the Almighty will be thrown down. But when? When will these things be?"

"Yes," demanded the burly fisherman Jack recognized as Simon Peter. "What will be the sign of your coming?"

"And," Peter's slightly older, quieter brother Andrew inquired, "What will be the sign of the end of the age?"

At a gesture from Yeshua His followers sank down onto boulders or leaned against gnarled olive tree trunks.

"These are all good questions," Yeshua replied. "I am concerned that you not let anyone lead you astray. Because, you see, there will be those who come, pretending to be me, even saying, 'I am the Christ. Worship me.' Sadly, these imposters will deceive many."

"What else?" Andrew asked softly.

Yeshua's chin dipped toward his chest before replying. "You will hear about wars—many wars—and rumors of still more wars. Do not be alarmed. Everything I'm telling you must take place, but even so, the end is not yet. Nation will rise against nation and kingdom against kingdom."

Raising his left hand toward heaven Yeshua marked each digit lightly with a touch of his right index finger. "There will be famines...."

Another touch: "Earthquakes. But remember," He admonished. "This is like a woman in labor. Birth pangs begin long before the child is born—but they increase in frequency and intensity as the birth draws near."

Yeshua returned to enumerating the signs. "You will be delivered up to tribulation. They will put you to death— and you will be hated by all nations for my name's sake."

NEVER FORGET

There is such intensity in Yeshua's words, Jack thought. *Wars, famines, earthquakes, tribulation and persecution…all happening more often as time goes by, and getting worse and worse. It's almost too much to take in!*

As if in answer to Jack's unspoken prayer, a vagrant breeze curled over the top of the Temple Mount and into the valley beneath. The swirl of air brought with it a veil of dust, obscuring Jack's view of Yeshua and His disciples. When the sky cleared, auto horns blared and the black bulk of the Dome of the Rock reappeared.

Enough to ponder for one lesson, Jack thought. *More than enough.*

---------------------- ✡ ✡ ✡ ----------------------

Tabitha Vanderhorst was among the last to visit Yad Vashem. Her journalism credentials granted her permission to film the memorial to holocaust victims.

Dodi had been right. Her text to Jack Garrison spoke of heartbreak and the terrible loss of an entire generation of people like Dodi.

Jack read the message to Dodi, who after a moment, agreed to allow the correspondent to film her testimony even as the plague of Covid-19 spread.

The flood of tourists traveling to Israel dried up to a trickle, and then evaporated within days of the announced shut down. Local shops in every quarter were shuttered. Small neighborhood grocery stores remained open, but

were subject to strict controls. The ultra-religious neigh-
borhoods in Jerusalem that ignored the social distancing
requirements were blockaded, as cases of the plague swept
through their communities.

Within Dodi's enclosed garden walls, the drama and
danger of the Corona plague seemed very distant.

Jack's cell phone buzzed as he and Bette shared tea and
wedding plans with the aged artist. Jack glanced at his
screen "It's Tabitha."

"Go ahead and take it," Dodi encouraged. "Ask her
to come by."

Jack answered. "Shalom."

Tabitha's voice sounded excited. "I'm headed back to
the states before the U.S. closes all travel. I'd like to record
Dodi today, if possible."

Within twenty minutes the bell at Dodi's gate rang. Jack
ushered Tabitha into Dodi's sanctuary. Dodi's works of art
were on display in secure glass cases. Blossoms overflowed
pots. Tangled wisteria vines climbed up trellises, and purple
blooms filled the air with fragrance.

Tabitha carried a tripod and a camera. She would film
the interview on her own. She sat beside Bette and set up
the equipment. The reporter fixed her attention on the
famed Israeli artist.

Beneath her broad, pale blue sun hat, and dark glasses,
Dodi turned her face toward the young woman.

"I came to Israel to write about archaeology, Middle
East politics and finally: you—the greatest Israeli artist."

Tabitha explained. "I fear you will be the last interview I have. I fly out tonight. Last flight to America."

Dodi, in her soft, melodious French accent, replied to the clink of Tabitha's china cup. "So you are caught in the whirlwind of the plague as well? Picked up and blown back to the states for quarantine?"

"Tabitha is lucky," Jack interjected. "Flying directly home to Los Angeles. New York is overrun with Corona virus cases. They expect New York and Jersey airports to be closed by tomorrow."

Dodi remarked, "Then this is truly a war. I thought as much."

Bette added, "Nothing like this since all the planes were grounded…."

Jack nodded. "This may be the 9-11 moment of this generation, I fear. The whole world is closing."

Dodi sighed. "Every generation must have their moment of tragedy; a day when everything changes. For me as a young wife and mother in Paris, it was September 29, 1939, when the Nazis attacked Poland and the World War began."

Tabitha glanced around the garden and turned on the camera. "This is what I wanted to interview you about. I have titled the article "Beauty from the Ashes." For the Sunday section. People need to hear. Need to remember. They are all forgetting. You were in a concentration camp. Such suffering, and yet, look at what you have accomplished." Tabitha swept her hand around the space. "I want you to tell your story. I've been to Yad Vashem. The children. You're right. We can never know. I'm sorry for the last minute intrusion. I just never expected...."

Dodi nodded. "Neither did we expect. None of us expected it. The plague." She paused. "Are we speaking of the past war? The war of Hitler against Israel and against every Christian? To rule the world? Or are we speaking of the present war? Today's war? Also a war to rule the world. The spiritual warriors are the same, though the game is a little different now."

Tabitha frowned and considered Dodi's words. "I was thinking of the World War you lived through. World War Two. Before there was Israel. Before you had a place to call home."

"Well, then," Dodi mused. "The facts of that terrible time are well known. The players? The Nazi press was the first to promote the downfall of democratic nations. German news was called The Ministry of Propaganda. Repeating constant lies, they convinced the people of Germany that the only truth tellers wore swastika armbands, and marched in goose steps, and smashed the windows of Jewish shops. They closed the churches, you know. People let them close their churches."

Tabitha turned on the camera and took notes as she spoke. "Go on, please."

"So am I speaking of then? 1938? Or am I speaking of now?" Dodi asked.

"Then. Your life."

"My life. Then I am speaking of both yesterday and

tomorrow, young lady. For you must write that this old woman has a clear and present warning for this time and this world. I see now that what happened in my youth is once again happening in this time. The demons of hell have laid in wait until all in my generation passed away. And now they are rising up from the sea to find habitation among the new generation."

Tabitha's expression looked suddenly pained. She blinked in horror. Color drained from her face.

Bette leaned forward in alarm. "Are you alright?"

"Yes. Yes. It's just that—the phrase Dodi used. That demons were rising from the sea?"

Bette encouraged her. "What is it?"

She hesitated. All eyes were on her.

Dodi said quietly, "Oh, yes. If we could have seen the dark spiritual creatures all around the world. Swarming like vultures. As it was in 1938, so it is in this generation. And we did not expect what happened. We did not expect it to sweep across nations. Nor did we believe it could come with such unreasoning violence. 'The evil beast has risen from the sea,' we said."

Tabitha cleared her throat. "I literally saw something like you are describing. December 26—on the Persian Gulf—I watched the solar eclipse rise over the Gulf. So strange. As it rose, it looked like the horns of an evil beast emerging from the sea." She held up her left hand, revealing an engagement ring. "My fiancé had expected we would see the corona of the sun. The sun's corona is like an engagement ring, he told me later. But the look of the sun rising from the sea that morning was more like a horned beast. Evil. So he did not propose to me until later."

Jack leaned back in his chair. "I read somewhere that the scientists who first named the corona virus back in 1986, named it after the look it had under a microscope. Like the sun's corona during an eclipse." He shrugged. "Someone once said, everything means something."

Dodi leaned back and sighed. "Ah. Yes."

Tabitha shrugged. "Just an eclipse. The moon over the sun, making it look like the head of a beast with horns. It frightened me, honestly. But still—just an eclipse."

Dodi tilted her head. "It is written: 'There shall be signs in the heavens.' In the 1930s we also saw evil signs. The desecration of churches and the burning of synagogues. The euthanasia of the elderly. Abortion of those whom the Aryans considered impure or defective. There were those in the church and among nations who might have spoken, but they did not. And so the story of mass destruction moves from being an enormous global catastrophe to become my own personal tragedy. I am only one small person. Only one who survived and rose up from the ashes among the six million who did not."

For two hours Dodi recounted her story, holding the journalist and all in the circle of those garden walls, enthralled. By the time Dodi's story came to an end, Tabitha Vanderhorst had only a few minutes to take photographs before she was whisked away to catch her flight back to America.

———————————————   ✡ ✡ ✡   ———————————————

Jack and Lev sat outdoors on a stone bench on the grounds of the Garden Tomb. Because of restrictions placed on travel by the virus crisis, the paths, normally crowded with pilgrims and tourists, were strangely empty.

Jack recounted his vision of Yeshua teaching on the Mount of Olives, instructing about His return and about the end of the age. "And then it stopped," he concluded. "I went home and read the rest for myself. Matthew twenty-four, right? So then I stayed awake all night, wondering what was left."

"Meaning?" Lev asked, sipping from a bottle of water.

"Meaning—what's left to happen? Before Jesus returns, I mean. Aren't twenty centuries of wars and earthquakes and famines enough?"

Lev nodded. "More than enough. And you know I've thought about it a lot myself. But listen, Jack, you already know that I believe we're in the last days, yes? There had to be an Israel again—and that happened in 1948. People used to bring up the idea that a generation of forty years from Israel's independence could not elapse without Jesus' return—but here we are now, more than seventy years later."

"So what does that mean?"

Lev shrugged. "The four hundred years that we Jews spent in Egypt is referred to in scripture as 'four generations.' By that calculation, each generation is a hundred years, not forty."

"Yes, but…."

Holding aloft a warning palm, Lev continued. "And some people say the generational countdown could not begin until Israel possessed the Temple Mount again."

"1967."

Lev nodded.

"And what…." Jack hesitated to complete his question, as if afraid to hear the response. "And what do you say?"

Lev waved toward the Temple Mount. "Where's the Temple of HaShem?" he said.

"The very issue that brought me to Israel," Jack concurred. "Rebuilding a Jewish temple on the Muslim's holy site is liable to be—No," he corrected himself, *"will be* the most divisive, the most inflammatory action in the world! Do you think that is a requirement for Jesus' to return?"

"I think…." Lev paused and grimaced. "I think something of enormous prophetic significance happened when the U.S. moved its embassy to Jerusalem. I think the last, best offering of land for a Palestinian state means something. I think that if we see the Temple standing there where it belongs," Lev waved toward the Temple Mount, "then Jesus will soon be setting His foot there." Lev completed the encompassing arch by indicating the Mount of Olives. "But do I think the Temple *has* to be rebuilt first?"

he said, repeating Jack's question. "No—I think Jesus could come tonight."

"But doesn't the Bible say that no man knows the day or the hour?"

"Yes, emphatically so," Lev agreed. "And no one should be setting a specific date. 'Like a thief in the night,' Paul says in I Thessalonians. But then he goes on to say this to his believing friends: 'But you, brothers, are not in darkness, so that this day should surprise you as a thief.'"

Jack felt his head swimming. "So what's the answer then? What?"

"We need a break," Lev said, laughing. "But when we pick up again we can talk about Jesus' return *and* about a coming wedding."

"Alright, Pastor! How's *that* gonna work?"

"It's a mystery—but it will, I promise."

✿ ✿ ✿

The teakettle whistled shrilly from Dodi's kitchen. Dodi looked toward Jack. "Tea kettles sound so much like train whistles, don't you think? Hello and goodbye. A lonely sound, if it catches one off guard."

"Not today," Jack replied. "I brought lemon bars and oolong tea and brown sugar lumps. It's hello for us today."

Dodi made as if to rise and fetch the brew. Jack put his hand on her frail shoulder. "I'll get it."

He made up the tray with her favorite, blue floral

Meissen china cups and teapot. When he returned with a plate of lemon bars, she was dozing. He lightly clattered the cups to gently awaken her.

"Oolong," Dodi inhaled deeply. "And lemon bars from the patisserie. I smell them. It reminds me of Paris when I was a young woman with your grandfather, and when your mother was an infant."

"Can anything taste as good as something from a Paris bakery?" Jack poured her tea, a little less than full lest she spill it.

"There was this little shop on the Left Bank. Very near the American bookshop; a cluttered place where the American writers always gathered to read aloud and talk about politics and plots. What was the name of it? A jumble of piles of old books surrounding scruffy American writers and artists who we know now were perhaps the most famous writers of their era. Hemingway and F. Scott Fitzgerald. I met them both. But I don't remember the name of the bookshop."

"Shakespeare and Company?"

"Yes. I think that's it. A messy, wonderful place. And just around the corner was the patisserie. Lemon bars sweet and tart and so rich you could eat them just a tiny bite at a time and make it last an hour."

Jack inhaled the fragrance of the oolong. "Funny to think of you at Shakespeare and Company. All before the war."

"Before France fell. Before the Nazis marched in. I have not ever returned to Paris since the day I carried your mother to the orphanage run by two spinster American sisters. Rose and Betsy Smith. They lived in a big house behind a gate. Number Five, Rue de la Huchette. Missionaries from California who came after the First World War to care for orphans. Then later, when the war began and it seemed that France would be over run—when our Jewish children were in danger and there was no place we could take them that was safe—I heard of them. They became like grandmothers to the Jewish children in their care. I knew my baby girl would be safe with them."

Jack leaned in closer. "Mamma didn't know the details of her rescue. So, of course I never knew."

Dodi's unseeing eyes gazed into a distant memory. "And I have not spoken of it. Maybe couldn't revisit it. Until now. With you. You see, to give up my beautiful baby to save her life. It was not just farewell. It was the tearing of one's soul. Hard to speak of even now."

"We don't have to."

"I think we should. Jack, some details you should know about your life. About how our little girl—your mother—was saved and survived, and so how you came to exist. Yes. Two spinster sisters. Paris. Number Five, Rue de la Huchette. A place of grief and a place of great relief. Knowing she was safe. We all knew that Betsy and Rose would die to keep our children safe. It was a difficult time. A time when every train whistle screamed the anguish of our breaking hearts. Loaded with children—our only true treasures—as they rolled out of Gare du Nord."

An hour passed. The tea grew tepid. Dottie shared the rest of her story. Jack suspected she left out the most terrible details of her capture and survival in the Nazi killing ground. She spoke about her rescue and return, and the war for Israel's survival in 1947 and 1948.

"And some who survived the death camps arrived here, had a rifle put in their hands, and then died fighting for this Jewish homeland." She drew a long breath. "You would think we would all be used to saying goodbye. But though you may expect it, you never get used to it." She placed her blue flowered cup on the tray. "I tell you this today because you are taking your beautiful bride to Paris on your honeymoon. And I wanted you to know. What happened in Paris is the reason there must be an Israel. There must always, always be an Israel."

3

THE WEDDING

Lev and Jack sat beside the gnarled trunk of their favorite olive tree on the Mount of Olives. Both had the obligatory face masks pulled down around their chins so they could sip their iced coffee. "Required, not required," Jack grumbled as hazelnut-flavored shaved ice dripped in his mask. "Changes every other day."

"I know," Lev commiserated. "And consider the issue with the ultra-orthodox who refused the mask ordinance right from the outset because of their beards. Then the Mea Shearim orthodox neighborhood had the highest rate of new infections, so the rabbis told their flocks to just stay home. *Oy gevalt*! It's a mess!"

"Do you think this virus is a plague? Like a biblical plague? And does it have anything to do with prophecy?" Jack asked.

"Jack," Lev retorted kindly. "You didn't ask to meet me the day before your wedding to discuss Covid-19, did you?"

"No," Jack admitted. "Lev, I'm so glad you're handling the ceremony for us. I mean—my last wedding wasn't Jewish."

"Neither were you," Lev laughed. "At least, you didn't know it then. But trust me, Jack. I won't let you mess it up—much. Besides, Benni is your Best Man, so you're covered! Anyway, a Messianic Jewish wedding is the perfect reflection of what all Christians believe—if they only knew their heritage."

"You mean because the first miracle Yeshua performed was at a wedding?"

"That's true, but not what I meant this time. You asked me about the plague and prophecy. What if I told you that every wedding was designed to reflect prophecy—even with a point about where we're sitting right now."

After carefully taking another swallow of his slushy drink, Jack said, "'Fraid you lost me, Lev."

"You asked me what Yeshua said were the signs of His return, yes? How to know when to expect His foot to touch right here?" Lev tapped the toe of his hiking boot on the gravel path. "The most definite thing He said was, 'Since you don't know exactly when I'm coming back, you need to be ready all the time.'"

"I get that—but how's that connect to weddings?"

"Yeshua used the imagery of a Jewish wedding to teach about His return. In this particular wedding story, the bride had ten bridesmaids. The tradition was, the bride knows her groom is preparing what will be their home, but the final decision on when everything is in readiness remains with the father of the groom. He's the one who says, 'Go get your bride.' Sound familiar?"

"Like when Jesus said, only the Father knows the day and the hour of Jesus' return?"

Lev agreed, took a sip of coffee, and continued. "That wasn't just a random comment. Jesus likened His return to a Jewish wedding. It is Yeshua saying, 'At some moment my Father will say that everything is complete, and then be ready, because I'm knocking on the bride's door to let the celebration begin!'"

"And back to the bridesmaids?" Jack queried.

"You remember: five wise, who had planned ahead, and had extra oil for their lamps. And five foolish: no extra oil, too late at night to buy more. The groom shows up and they're locked out of the party.

"Men and women," Lev continued, "are all created to be friends and lovers of God. We were never made for anything else. So here's Jesus, telling us that our relationship with God is meant to be the fundamental structure of our lives—but some don't live like it.

"Even the foolish bridesmaids had lamps. They had the *form* of being believers."

"Like Christians in name only?" Jack surmised.

"Got it. No oil means no power. If I call myself Christian but I live like the non-believers—if I don't allow

God to reign in my life—if I don't have the oil of the Holy Spirit supplying the energy in my spiritual life—then I risk being locked out of the party when Jesus, the Bridegroom, comes."

Jack looked stunned; impressed, but shocked. "And this is what *every* wedding of believers is supposed to reenact?"

"The Church is the Bride. Jesus is the Groom. The Father says to the Son: 'Now's the time. Go get her and bring her home.'

"We got betrothed two thousand years ago," Lev added. "The party can start *any* time now. What'd Paul say to the Romans? 'For our salvation is nearer now than when we first believed.'"

Jack sat for a moment, swirling his drink in its plastic cup. "Lev?" Jack inquired. "Will you repeat this for our wedding? I really want Bette to hear it while I'm looking into her face."

"You got it, brother. Count on it."

--------------------- ✡ ✡ ✡ ---------------------

Later that same night, Jack stood beside Eliyahu in King David's city. "Soon, you will be married," Eliyahu said. "You know, in our tradition, the bridegroom goes to build a home for his bride. This is what the Lord Jesus meant when He said, 'I am going to prepare a place for you.'"

"The Wedding Supper of the Lamb," Jack murmured, marveling. "I've learned it's all about Yeshua, the Groom, coming for His Bride, the Church."

As moonlight flooded the City of David archeological dig, Eliyahu explained, "This City of David is the true foundation of Jerusalem. This exact place on earth is the gate into the heavenly Jerusalem."

"Then Jerusalem is not as the world sees?"

"Indeed not. Listen to the words of the prayer which Yeshua taught his disciples: 'Thy kingdom come, Thy will be done on earth, as it is in Heaven.' You see, Jack, it is written that the heavenly Jerusalem will come down to earth. The Kingdom of the Almighty, perfect in beauty and in peace—Shalom—will be here. Right here in this place. This land, undivided, is reserved by the Almighty as the setting for His throne room."

Jack scanned the deep shadows of the dig, imagining the days when King David walked through the streets of the ancient city. "Time is short," he said.

"Time is *up*," Eliyahu answered.

Looking toward the stars, Jack thought for a moment he caught the golden glow of the great city of God waiting to enter the broken world. "We are so shattered."

"I will tell you a secret about the name of Jerusalem in Hebrew. The root of the name is Shalom. You think shalom means, 'peace,' but it means so much more than that. It means also, 'wholeness,' to be made complete and whole.

"So its very name says it cannot be divided; must not be divided." Jack grasped the beginning of the importance of Jerusalem as the undivided capital of Israel.

"And there is so much more. *Yerushalem* is the name of the

earthly city. It is singular. But there is a word in the *tanakh* that is used when we speak of the Heavenly City joined with the earthly one. We call it *Yerushalayim*. Plural. The two are joined, you see. Heaven holds up a mirror of what will soon be; when the heavenly Jerusalem comes down."

Jack felt a chill run through him as understanding dawned. "The two are one. 'Thy kingdom come on *earth* as it *is* in heaven.'"

"And this is why the enemies of Israel fight so hard on earth to divide the city God has called His own."

"Pray for the peace; the wholeness; the Shalom of Yerushalayim."

"So, you see the light." Eliyahu waved his hand and the vision of a majestic palace rose from the rubble. "It is coming. It is real."

"How will I ever understand the depth of the Word of God?" Jack felt his knees grow weak. He sank down. Eliyahu lifted him up. "Everything means something. Even the Hebrew name of Jerusalem says it must never be divided!"

"One day you will see it all clearly," Eliyahu offered comfortingly. "Indeed, it is enough for now to know that everything means something. There are four layers of scripture. The first is the surface: the plain meaning of the text. The second goes a little deeper: you see a hint that there is something more to the text. The third level is the level into which you must inquire. You must research to grasp the deeper meaning. And the fourth level contains the deepest of the deep secrets within the text—and all these levels are interconnected; they are alive!"

Jack drank his words in deeply. "I will need eternity to understand it all. How can a mere mortal mind grasp this?"

"One day when the City of the Great King of the Universe is revealed, you will understand. Meanwhile, as you live here, the Holy Spirit of God is a lamp, lighting the path. The Word of God is alive! Its wisdom a universe of many facets." He took Jack's arm. "So we must get back. The dawn is coming."

☆ ☆ ☆

Jack gazed serenely over the setting of his wedding. Lev and Benni, Ron Silver and his wife, sat beside Jack, awaiting the arrival of the bride's limo and a mere handful of guests who would be present.

"What do you think, Benni?" Jack asked Bette's brother, "Will your sister like this?"

"She will. She will say it's mystical. She will say it's like something out of Lord of the Rings, I think."

The secret of where the wedding would be held had been kept from Bette. She knew the date and the time, but using the Rachaelim winery location, one of her favorite places in all of Israel, for the ceremony, was still a secret.

Twinkle lights winked like fireflies in the ancient oak tree at the winery. Torches burned brightly along the path leading up to the wedding canopy. Strings of café lights were draped across the circle which, in normal times, would have held several hundred guests.

Most of Israel was shut down because of the pandemic. Large gatherings were forbidden. As the contagion spread, the restrictions became even more draconian.

The Israeli tourist trade was completely shut down. Shops in Jerusalem were shuttered. Masks remained required for all public excursions to the grocery store or other necessary shopping.

No more than a handful of people could gather together for any occasion. And yet, Jack and Bette would not be thwarted.

Bette whittled down the wedding guest list to the permitted small size. Five bridesmaids included Lev's wife, Katy, but the others were young women Bette had served with in the Israeli Defense Forces. Dodi rounded out the very small wedding party.

A banquet was to be served in the wine cave after the ceremony.

The headlights of Bette's stretch limousine turned off the road and onto the long gravel drive.

A rush of excitement surged through Jack. So this was it. A new life beginning after he had once thought his life had come to an end. He quietly prayed, "Thank you Lord for letting me live to see this joyful moment."

Benni, who was the sole musician, readied his clarinet and struck up a haunting melody: *Hana-Ava Babanot.* The Fairest of Maidens.

THE WEDDING

The scene was set, and even if there had been hundreds to celebrate with them, Jack's only focus was on Bette. For him there was no one else in the world. Surely angels rejoiced in the stars above them, but Jack felt that he and Bette were the only ones on the hilltop.

Lev stepped forward to meet the bride's wedding party. The vehicle pulled up and the door opened.

Dodi emerged first. Lev took her arm and stepped aside as the pale blue-clad bridesmaids, each carrying a small, clay, oil lamp, got out. They lit their lamps by the flame of the torch, then lined up to escort the bride.

Bette's white lace gown, embroidered with tiny pearls, shimmered in the torchlight as she stepped out of the limo. A lace veil was draped across the top of her head, framing her face.

Jack's breath caught at the sight of her radiant beauty. He could barely breathe as the bridesmaids preceded her up the path.

After taking Dodi and Katy to their seats, Lev summoned Jack and Bette to join him beside a lectern on which rested a parchment document. Together they signed the *ketubah;* the marriage contract.

Jack and Lev stood together under the *chuppah*; a canopy formed of prayer shawls, and festooned with garlands of roses. Benni's clarinet echoed across the vineyard as he launched into *Erev Shel Shoshanim*, Evening of Roses. The IDF women accompanied Bette seven times around the canopy. After the seventh circuit, they brought her to stand at Jack's side.

Lev remarked, "Jack, you must now veil your bride. Unlike our ancestor, Jacob, who was tricked at his first wedding, you have now seen that this is truly your beloved. It is to the woman standing before you to whom you pledge your life in exchange for hers."

As Jack let the lace folds fall gently across Bette's face he whispered, "I hope Lev hurries. I'm not ready to stop looking at you—forever."

Lev spoke to the assembly as being witnesses to this contract. He charged the guests with the responsibility of aiding and assisting the newly wedded couple in making their marriage solid and unbreakable.

The couple exchanged rings and committed themselves to each other's care.

Then lifting a glass of wine brought to him by Benni, Lev said, "Blessed are You, Lord God, King of the Universe, Who gives us the fruit of the vine, and with it, commands us to sanctify this marriage."

From that beginning, Lev spoke of how appropriate it was that the first miracle performed by Yeshua of Nazareth was the supernatural exchange of water for wine for the wedding at Cana. "No one should ever try to tell you that Jesus did not claim to be God," Lev warned. "In that very first mysterious act, Yeshua identified Himself with 'the King of the Universe, Who gives us the fruit of the vine.'"

With the blessing of the wine as the first, Lev proceeded to proclaim the remainder of the seven traditional blessings, concluding with, "Blessed are You, Lord God, King of the Universe, who created joy and gladness, groom and bride, mirth, song, delight and rejoicing, love and harmony and peace and companionship. Blessed are You, Lord, Who gladdens the groom with his bride."

Extending the wine glass to the couple, Lev gestured for Jack to offer it to Bette. Lifting a corner of the veil, she took a sip, then returned the glass to Jack, who drained it.

From Dodi's hands Lev received a cloth bag into which he enclosed the glass. Laying it on its side in front of the couple, he said to Jack. "No one else will ever share this cup. It is a bond between you two forever.

There was a muted but audible crunch as Jack smashed the glass with his heel, and the congregation erupted into shouts of "Mazel tov!"

"Is that it?" Jack asked.

"I think you better kiss the bride," Lev scolded.

Lifting the veil and kissing Bette's shining, upturned lips, produced another cry of "Mazel tov," from the assembly, and then Benni broke into *Dodi Li*, My Beloved is Mine, and I am His.

And the ceremony—but not the rejoicing—was over.

✡ ✡ ✡

Bette changed from her wedding dress to traveling clothes. She embraced Benni farewell. "Be a good boy. Mind Lon. I will bring you something from Paris."

The boy buried his face against his sister. "Be careful," he said.

Jack wondered if the boy's parting words were a warning, or only a prayer? Perhaps both.

Bette hugged Dodi tightly as Jack waited by the door of the limo. "We are truly family now," Bette said in Hebrew.

Dodi replied, "You are the granddaughter I have always longed for." Dodi kissed her cheek. "I know you have been thinking of your family today. I want you to know, your mother and father would be so proud and happy, my dear."

Bette held the old woman a long moment and replied softly, "Of everyone here, I know you understand how much they have been in my thoughts."

Dodi held Bette's hands, "I understand. There is never an occasion of joy in my life in which my family has not been a part of my thoughts. And their absence is a shadow amidst my joy. But I learned early in life that I must choose joy. Choose to go on with my head up and my gaze forward. May the Lord bless you and Jack with a great family; a generation of children who will change the world for the Kingdom of God."

"And may you live long, to see your great grandchildren," Lev interjected. "Omaine."

As the limo drove down the twisting dirt lane toward the main road, Bette looked back and waved a long goodbye.

At last she turned to Jack and leaned her cheek against his chest. He breathed her in. Her scent was intoxicating to him. "Mrs. Garrison." He kissed her gently and she melted into his embrace.

Smiling up at him she said, "Thank you, Jack. You've given me something I never thought would be mine again. A family. Dodi. A real grandmother."

"It's my turn to thank you. I never thought I could love anyone like I love you. Beyond words. Not ever. But here you are in my arms."

"And a honcymoon in Paris!" She laughed. "Now, will you tell me where we are staying?"

"No," he refused. "It's a surprise, like the wedding location. I've been working on this for weeks. You're going to have to trust me."

The airport in Tel Aviv was almost deserted, due not only to the late hour of their departure, but tourists unwilling to undergo fourteen days of quarantine in Israel had canceled their trips to the Holy Land.

It seemed to Jack that the security screening was more stringent than usual.

Required to wear masks, they boarded the nearly empty plane to Paris, and were upgraded to First Class.

When the aircraft lifted off Jack took a deep breath and pulled Bette close against him. She fell asleep within minutes.

He did not dare move for fear of waking her.

Gazing out the window at the countless stars, he silently prayed a prayer of thanks and blessing over his wife.

His determination to protect her from everything—from

anyone who might threaten her—was intense. She had been through so much. He prayed that he could be her fortress.

As she slept against his arm, he felt the nearness of angels watching over them. At last, a smile of contentment on his lips, he allowed himself to finally and fully relax.

4

CYRUS THE GREAT

The drumming of the airplane engines morphed into a persistent vibration that lulled Jack to sleep soon after the El Al flight left the runway. The travel time was five hours, and after the wedding celebration, and the drive to the air-port, and the navigating of security—it was already three in the morning.

Eliyahu's voice reached into Jack's unconscious. "Can't I just sleep?" Jack complained.

"You *are* sleeping," Eliyahu corrected. "I promise you will still be rested when you awaken. Walk with me."

Jack and Eliyahu emerged from a mist outside a large, grandly carved stone building. "Where are we?" Jack asked.

"In Persia," was the response. "Just outside the halls of

Cyrus, who is not yet, but will soon be called, 'the Great.'
With the king are Jewish counselors whom Cyrus honors:
Ezra the Scribe, and Daniel the Prophet of the Lord. Put
your right hand upon my left shoulder," Eliyahu instructed
Jack, who obliged. "Now we will enter into the presence of
the king. This is his first year as ruler over all of Persia. But
first, what is that in your other hand?"

Jack opened his palm and examined a newly minted
gold coin. "This has the likeness of King Cyrus and the
president of the United States together. Some are calling
this president a modern day Cyrus."

Eliyahu smiled slightly. "Put the coin in your pocket.
The connection between the first Cyrus and the latter man
is their link to Jerusalem and Israel. Listen carefully and
you will understand why these two faces are cast together
in gold. Now hold tight. This meeting links the past with
the present. It will show you the meaning of the prophecy
concerning the Temple and Jerusalem."

Jack held tightly to the prophet's cloak as Eliyahu
stepped over the invisible threshold. In an instant they were
in the splendor of King Cyrus' palace.

In a great hall, half as big as a football field, a forest
of enormous marble columns rose up from a patterned
floor of blue lapis and black onyx. Ornate bronze sconces
held torches that lit the space. Smoke rose up and half-ob-
scured the brightly colored ceiling. The height of the pillars
dwarfed Jack and Eliyahu, and the dozens of courtiers waiting outside the King's Hall of Judgment.

CYRUS THE GREAT

Eliyahu gestured toward the white alabaster carvings on either side of the broad steps leading into the throne room. Images depicted men of every race and nation in the vast Persian Empire. All were bearing gifts, representing the bounty of their nations, paid in tribute to King Cyrus.

It was, Jack mused, a contract in stone of many vassal nations unified within the mighty Empire of Persia. Sculpted faces gazed forward; eyes focused only on the great king; supreme ruler of all the ancient world.

"Why have we come today?" Jack asked.

Eliyahu seemed to study the details of the wall carvings as he slowly climbed the steps. "You must step into the story. You are a witness to the hinge of ancient history. This is the moment of Jeremiah's prophetic fulfillment. This is the moment of Cyrus about which the prophet Isaiah declared. The Lord has put it into the heart of King Cyrus to make a proclamation throughout all his realm in order to fulfill the word of the Lord spoken to Jeremiah about the return of the Jews to Israel and the rebuilding of the Temple in Jerusalem."

Two enormous bronze doors opened at the urging of a quartet of burly bodyguards. The two visitors from another era passed from the outer reception hall into the very throne room of Cyrus. Here the walls and ceiling, covered by gold leaf, seemed to radiate light from within.

Cyrus the King was flanked by two live, tawny, menacing lions, restrained by golden chains. The monarch known as the King of Kings sat upon royal blue, brocade cushions on an elevated ivory throne. A dozen officers and advisers were near, waiting for the King's command.

"Cyrus seems to be a very young man," Jack whispered to Eliyahu.

"No need to whisper." Eliyahu smiled from behind his grizzled beard. "They can neither see nor hear us. Cyrus is a man whose heart is turned toward the Lord God, Jehovah."

"Who are the men seated to his right?" Jack studied a serious-looking, dark-haired man, and an elder Jew with a scroll open before him.

"The first is Ezra the Jew, who has the favor and friend-ship of King Cyrus. The elder with the scroll is Daniel."

Jack nodded. He had studied the book of Ezra and knew that Ezra was the man appointed to rebuild the Temple in Jerusalem. Daniel, known for his wisdom, was renowned among the wisest in the land. Jack gripped the fabric of Eliyahu's cloak tighter.

King Cyrus spoke to Daniel, "Show me, O Daniel, Prophet of the Most High God of the Jews, what you have found in the scroll concerning me!"

Daniel rose and carried the scroll to Cyrus, laying it open on a golden table before him. With a nod of his head, Daniel spoke: "King Cyrus, your name was written in the Tanach, in the book of Isaiah, one hundred fifty years before you were born."

King Cyrus leaned in to study the Hebrew letters that

seemed to glow, golden, on the scroll. "Read the words of the prophet aloud to me."

Daniel's voice was strong and firm, resounding in the palace as he read the prophecy. "Thus says Hashem, your redeemer and the One Who formed you from the womb: I am Hashem, Who has made everything; and formed the earth of My own accord; who abrogates the omens of the stargazers and makes fools of the astrologers! Who makes wise men retreat and makes their knowledge foolish. Who confirms the words of His servant and fulfills the counsel of His messengers. Who says of Jerusalem, 'It shall be settled,' and of the cities of Judah, 'They shall be built up, and I will rebuild its ruins....' Who says of Cyrus, 'He is My shepherd, he will fulfill all My desires,' to say of Jerusalem, 'It shall be built,' and of the Temple, 'It shall be established.'"

Daniel paused as King Cyrus contemplated the words of Isaiah.

The king rested his chin in hand. He looked up. "Is there more?"

Daniel smiled. "The promise of blessing upon you, King Cyrus," he responded.

The monarch snapped his finger and commanded Ezra, "I who am King Cyrus, written of in the prophecy, declare this. We shall make a proclamation on this day throughout the realm and commit it to writing."

All eyes were on the King. A scribe picked up his stylus to record the King's command on the smooth, soft surface of a clay tablet.

Cyrus paused a moment until he was certain that all were listening. He motioned for Ezra to come and stand before him

His deep voice resounded in the great hall: "This is what Cyrus, King of Persia says: The Lord, the God of Heaven, has given me all the kingdoms of earth and has appointed me to build a Temple for Him at Jerusalem in Judah." Cyrus fixed his gaze on Ezra. "To anyone of His people among you. May his God be with him, and let him go up to Jerusalem in Judah and build the Temple of the Lord, the God of Israel; the God who is in Jerusalem. And the people of any place where His survivors may now be living are to provide them with silver and gold, with goods and livestock, and with freewill offerings for the Temple of God in Jerusalem!"

Cyrus stretched out his gleaming scepter to Ezra, who touched the lion's-head cap.

The king remarked, "So, Ezra. So have I spoken, and so it will be done."

Tears ran down Ezra's cheeks. He bowed his head and placed his hand over his heart in a gesture of thanks. "The gratitude of the whole people of Israel is yours forever, your Majesty. May your name live forever, O mighty King Cyrus, for the kind favor you have shown to the children of Israel and to the people of the God of Israel."

Cyrus turned his attention to Daniel, "Read the rest of the words concerning me."

Daniel continued, reading the passage Jack recognized

from Isaiah chapter forty-five. "Thus said HaShem to His anointed one, to Cyrus, whose right hand I have grasped, to subdue nations before him, that I might loosen the loins of kings and make them fear, to open doors before him, and that gateways not be shut. I will go before you and straighten twisting paths; I will smash copper doors and sever iron bolts; and I will grant you the treasures of darkness and hidden riches of secret places, in order that you should know that I am HaShem Who has proclaimed your name—I, the God of Israel—for the sake of My servant Jacob and Israel, My chosen one; I have proclaimed you by name; I dubbed you, though you did not know me, in order that those from east and west would know that there is nothing besides me.'"

Again, Daniel left off reading. It was enough. Jack saw the light in the eyes of Cyrus. He understood. Jack whispered, "From east to west. The west. America?"

Cyrus answered Daniel: "I am also a servant of the One True God. He is the Great King of Heaven and Earth. It is a small thing I offer to Him in thanks."

Eliyahu and Jack stood beside King Cyrus, Daniel, and Ezra as the treasures stolen from the Temple of Jerusalem by the Babylonians were brought out of the treasury and displayed on tables in the anteroom beside the Hall of Judgment. Cyrus instructed his treasurer, "Mithredath, stack the gold and silver on separate tables. Take an inventory of all these things belonging to the Temple of the Lord which Nebuchadnezzar had carried away from Jerusalem and then had placed in the vile temple of his god.

"Sheshbezar," Cyrus instructed an assistant, "Call out the articles and write down the inventory."

The process of inventorying and wrapping the booty for the long journey home took hours. Cyrus ordered a feast to be brought to himself and Ezra and the workmen.

"Of silver dishes," Sheshbezar reported, "one thousand. Of gold dishes, thirty. Of silver pans, twenty-nine. Of golden bowls, thirty. Of matching silver bowls, four hundred ten."

In all, there were five thousand, four hundred articles of gold and silver which were sorted, wrapped, and crated, as the king observed with an expression of great pleasure on his face.

Cyrus asked Ezra, "Are all the family heads of Judah and Benjamin, and the Priests and Levites, prepared?"

"Yes, your Majesty," Ezra answered. "Everyone whose heart God has moved—we are prepared to go up and rebuild the house of the Lord in Jerusalem."

Cyrus smiled through his thick beard. "All who are called by the Lord are ready. All but one, I suppose."

Ezra shook his head, questioning the King, "Who is left?"

Cyrus patted his own chest. "Myself. Oh, how I long to see the Temple of the One True God when it is complete! Yes. The Lord has put that in my heart. But I shall not see it. Therefore, Ezra, you must be my eyes. You must write down all the events of this great enterprise and send messengers to me to report your progress."

"I will. I promise I will not leave out any detail of our holy assignment."

"I have heard a whisper in the night. In the darkest hour—when the nightingale sings outside my window—I heard a voice like a song, and smelt the scent of flowers I have never smelled before."

"What is it, your Majesty?"

"It is the voice of He who dwells in the Temple of Jerusalem. He has told me a secret. And I shall tell you, Daniel and Ezra, my friends."

The king studied the crates filled with treasure for a long moment. "He says to me that one distant day the Temple in Jerusalem will rise, and again the treasures of old will be brought forth from the gloom where they lie hidden. And the eyes of mankind shall see the revelation of what was great glory. But we, you and I, will then be but shadows in the memories of mankind. New eyes shall behold these wonders. All this," the king spread his arms wide, "is but a rehearsal of all that is to come. Do you understand?"

"A rehearsal," Ezra repeated, as the boxes were lifted and carried toward the wagons outside the door.

"I shall not see the Temple you build. I will sleep until a time to come. This is but the first enactment of a great ingathering of the children of Israel. The Temple you build will once again be torn down. There shall be centuries of turmoil and a time of great trouble for your people. Then, at the end of days, as Isaiah and Jeremiah the prophets fore-told, they shall return to Israel from all the distant corners of the earth."

"Yes, Great King?"

"A man of great authority, whom many will call by my name, Cyrus, shall arise in a distant land. His voice shall resound across the nations like a trump of warning. Many shall hate him fiercely and seek his destruction. Yet, by his favor, and the favor of his nation, toward Israel and the Word of the Lord, Jerusalem will be restored—even as it is with the blessing of my kingdom that it is happening now. The Temple shall be rebuilt in that end time and then...."

"Then?"

"In that very time all that was predicted by the prophets shall come to pass. The Great King of Heaven and Earth shall appear and set his feet on the Mountain of the Lord."

"It is a beautiful vision, mighty king."

"Not all beautiful. But all is true." King Cyrus paused and exhaled deeply. His shoulders sagged as though he was suddenly exhausted. "I will see the Temple at the end, when everything old has passed away and eternity is just beginning. The once and future king will come indeed, and by my offering and honoring of His Temple I will also be remembered."

Jack stood, transfixed by the scene playing out before him. "The hinge of history," he said to Eliyahu. "I understand."

Eliyahu touched Jack's arm. "There is much more for

you to see. But it will be for another time. Until then, you must ponder what this means. Two faces on your golden coin. King Cyrus and the President of the United States. They lived thousands of years apart and yet both have impacted the return and restoration of the nation of Israel. Both have favored Jerusalem and both see in their lifetimes the fulfillment of prophecy."

The light of the golden throne room began to recede. Jack watched as Daniel, Ezra, and King Cyrus faded into the distance.

Winds roared in Jack's ears. He felt a force swirl around him, lifting him far beyond the boundaries of time and space. Silence fell. Unfamiliar stars shone above him. He floated above the earth as he held tightly to the prophet's cloak. And then his grip could hold no longer, and he fell back into untroubled, restorative sleep.

5

THE REIGN OF TERROR

Suitcases loaded on the luggage trolley, Jack and Bette emerged from Terminal Two of Charles de Gaulle Airport. Within five minutes of collecting their luggage they slipped into the back seat of a limo for the forty-five-minute ride into Central Paris.

"Can you tell me where you're taking me now?" Bette laughed.

"Okay. You know we're in France. Paris is the most romantic city on earth. It's our honeymoon. Where do you want to go?"

"You know I've never been to Disneyland. Disney Paris?"

"I can add that to our itinerary. Maybe after dinner at the Eiffel Tower, and lunch with Mona Lisa at the Louvre?"

The amused eyes of the driver looked at Jack in the rear

view mirror. "Perhaps we can keep the destination a secret from the lady, but *I* need to know where I am taking you."

Jack held a finger to his lips then passed a slip of paper through a slot in the plexiglass window. Their destination was written on it.

"Well done. I know this place, monsieur! May I assure the lady this is indeed the most romantic location on earth."

Bette slipped her arm through Jack's and raised her face to his for a lingering kiss.

The journey into the heart of the French capital was silent after that. Perhaps there were glimpses of the Eiffel Tower, or of Montmartre on the horizon, but neither Jack nor Bette noticed.

Bette's eyes were full of longing. She searched Jack's face, and touched his cheek, and whispered, "Truth is, I'll go wherever you're taking me."

The limo pulled up beside the River Seine and stopped. The driver waited a long moment for them to notice. "Monsieur. Madame. Pont Neuf, the New Bridge. It is the oldest bridge across the Seine, but several hundred years ago it was the newest bridge. So the name stuck. You have arrived."

Jack said quietly. "We're here. You can look now."

Pont Neuf was adorned by an enormous equestrian statue of King Henri IV. Pigeons roosted on his crown, and on the head of his rearing bronze horse. The current of the Seine swept through the pilings of the bridge. Blue sky reflected on the surface of the wide river.

Beyond the Eighteenth century buildings of the Palais de Justice, and the Gothic spire of Sainte-Chapelle Church, the unmistakable towers of Notre Dame Cathedral framed the island, known as Île de la Cité.

Jack paid the taxi driver and tipped him well. "Thanks."

"A perfect beginning, monsieur." The driver touched his hat to Bette, and remarked as he drove away, "Trust me. Better than Pirates of the Caribbean, madame."

Bette saluted, then stepped onto the quay overlooking the Seine and drank in the view. Down a flight of steep stone steps the boat of the Paris Fire Brigade was moored. Three firemen lounged on the deck of the fireboat.

Tied up to the quay just beyond the fire-fighting craft was a ninety-foot-long, black-lacquered, wooden canal barge. Chairs and a small dining table were on the deck. Red geranium blossoms spilled over their baskets dotted atop the pristine deck.

"Our view." Jack put his arm around Bette's shoulders.

"He's right. Better than Disneyland. But where is our hotel?"

"Hotel? There's no hotel here. "He gathered her into his arms and carried her down the stone steps onto the quay, and then crossed the gang plank onto the deck of the barge. He kissed her again. They descended the stairs into the salon of the boat where he laid her on the double berth. His voice was tender as he unbuttoned the top button of her red silk blouse and pressed his lips to her throat. "What do you think, Mrs. Garrison? Can you be happy sharing a too-small berth with a wan-na-be pirate?"

"Yes. Oh, so happy! But Jack? There's just one thing."

"Anything you want. Anything. Name it. I'll lasso the moon for you, like George Bailey."

"George Bailey? No. It's just that—we—we—darling, Jack. I think we left our luggage on the quay."

"Leave it," he said, then relenting added, "At least the bag with my cell phone in it. I don't expect to need it in Paris—period."

☼ ☼ ☼

Predawn light filtered through the porthole of the cabin. Jack could feel the morning arrive before he opened his eyes. For just a moment he forgot where he was.

Bette was curled up against him. Fragrant, warm and perfect, her breath was soft and even against his back. He didn't move for fear of waking her. She sighed and stirred, then whispered, "Jack?"

Softly he answered, "You awake?"

"Hmmm. You?"

"Sun's almost up. Morning's the only time of day it's quiet in Paris. The French stay up all night and sleep away half the day."

She stroked his neck and ran her fingers through his hair. "But you are an early riser, I see."

"Yes." He laughed, then turned over on the

narrow bunk. They lay together, face-to-face, smiling at one another.

At last Bette spoke in a languid voice. "Hungry?"

"Getting there."

"What do you want for breakfast?"

He pulled her closer. "You."

She traced his lips with her finger. "Funny. That's what I was going to say. Breakfast in bed?"

✡ ✡ ✡

After lockdown in Israel because of the plague, France seemed like a release from jail. Though there was a government edict requiring face coverings, the citizens of French took all official orders with an open disregard. The boulevards were less crowded than Jack had ever seen, but sidewalk cafes were filled with customers on every street.

As Jack stood in line to purchase elevator tickets to ascend the Eiffel Tower, there were masks, but no one seemed to pay attention to physical distancing.

In the back of the queue, someone coughed.

Bette's eyes widened. Long weeks of caution in Israel had an effect. She tugged his sleeve as they inched toward the ticket window. Smiling at him she asked, "Let's walk up?"

From the esplanade to the top of the tower there were one thousand, six hundred and sixty-five steps. It would have been nothing for a woman as fit as Bette, he thought proudly, but the sign indicated that tonight the stairs past the second level were closed.

Jack purchased the combination of stair and lift tickets from the second level to the top. Bette took the steps like she was walking on level ground. Jack, breathless, trailed along after her.

They lingered on the viewing platform of the second level. The view of Paris at night was spectacular, but Bette turned to look at the elevator doors every time they opened.

"What's up?" Jack asked. "This is supposed to be romantic. The lights of the city are out there. You're looking at the elevator."

"Probably nothing. Just my training I suppose. You'll think I'm paranoid. But—there were two guys in line behind us. Middle Eastern. Staring at me. Palestinian, maybe. Masks, and they spoke French, so I couldn't tell. Lebanese? Could even be Israeli from the look of their shirts. So out of place here. This is the Eiffel Tower after all. Romantic. Yes?"

"You think we're being watched?"

"No. Well, maybe. If we were being followed, not too much to worry about. They are overweight. Smoking. Not the type to hike up stairs and live to tell about it."

"And?"

"They bought the same admission you bought. Stairs and lift combination. They followed us up. I watched them behind us as we climbed. They were dying after about the first hundred steps. Leaning on the handrails. Breathing hard. Candidates for heart attacks. They couldn't even make it up the second hundred steps. Turned around and went back down."

"You think they'll buy lift tickets?"

"Only if they're following us."

At that, the elevator doors slid open. Two Middle Eastern men stood at the front of the packed lift. Their haggard eyes betrayed relief as they spotted Bette and Jack. They stepped off the lift just as Bette pushed past them and pulled Jack on. The doors closed, leaving the pursuers on the second level.

"So." Jack clasped Bette's hand.

"So." Bette answered.

The elevator reached the top of the observation deck. Jack quickly pulled Bette behind a steel girder to watch.

The next load of tourists spilled from the lift. The two men walked onto the deck, scanning the space, definitely looking for someone.

As they rounded the corner, Jack and Bette slipped back onto the elevator and returned undetected to the esplanade.

"The question is who?" Jack remarked as they hurried back to the boat by an alternate way.

"And why?"

"You scared?" Jack asked.

"Not a bit," Bette returned scornfully. "Cautious and prepared—but not scared. Besides," she added thoughtfully, "Perhaps I'm just too paranoid."

THE CYRUS MANDATE

✿ ✿ ✿

On the second morning after their arrival in Paris, the deck planks creaked under Jack's feet as he slipped out of the canal barge's bunk. At the sound Jack pivoted toward the bed to see if he had awakened Bette.

He had not. She was still sound asleep. A street lamp on the quayside surrendered to the coming of day. Its last beam pierced a galley porthole, illuminating Bette's face. A tiny smile was printed on her perfect lips. A lock of dark hair lay across her face; daring Jack to brush it aside.

He stood transfixed; staring at her—drinking her in.

I love this woman so much, he thought. *Thank you, God. I will never be able to deserve the mighty, unexpected blessings You have poured into my life—but I won't say no!*

Bette stirred under the sheets, turning on her side with a gentle, sighing breath.

Jack reached toward her shoulder, then stopped himself.

This gorgeous woman deserves the best I can be, he argued with himself. *A quick jog up the river and back, to balance all the rich Parisian food!* Stepping into sweats and running shoes, Jack slid open the hatch and emerged in the cool, pre-dawn air. A couple stretches and Jack was ready to go.

His route led up the steps past the fire boat. A trio of early risers—members of the Paris firefighters known as *Le Regiment de Sapeurs-Pompiers*—returned Jack's wave with uplifted coffee mugs.

Still no traffic on Parisian streets, Jack noticed. It was quiet enough to hear the ripples as the Seine lapped against the supporting piers of the bridges.

Jack jogged first north along the Left Bank, crossed the Pont des Arts toward the Louvre, then returned along the Right Bank to the eastern end of Pont Neuf. The bridge was actually two spans that converged on the tip of Île de la Cité.

At the place where the two arches met, Jack paused to draw breath beside the equestrian statue of King Henri IV—Good King Henri, as he was known. Leaning against the plinth and rising onto his toes to stretch out his leg muscles, Jack smiled as he peered down at the canal barge and the vision of Bette sleeping aboard it. The Seine's unhurried pilgrimage to the Atlantic drew Jack's eyes from the barge toward the Pont des Arts he had just crossed.

That's odd, he thought. *Why can't I see it? It didn't feel like that much of a run.* The back of Jack's neck prickled.

Here? he queried. *In Paris? On my honeymoon?*

"It is important," Eliyahu's words reassured him. "Pont des Arts hasn't been built yet. The year is 1792. Does that date mean anything to you?"

Before Jack could reply, central Paris was flooded with the brilliance of the noonday sun. From both banks of the river came shouting throngs of men and women, waving barrel staves and ax handles, sharpened pikes and red banners.

Dozens of rioters were barefoot. There was no recognizable uniform, but many wore red mob caps topped with—"The tricolor cockade of the French Revolution," Jack murmured.

"Exactly," Eliyahu agreed.

"But—but why show me this?"

"Watch," Eliyahu commanded.

The crashing human tide coalesced on Pont Neuf. Their shrieking drowned the voice of the river. Instinctively, Jack backed up from the statue to look toward the canal barge and Bette's safety. Of course, the boat wasn't there.

"Citizens!" a swarthy, sweating Parisian shouted over the tumult. "Down with all that is hateful! No more monarchy! No more honoring oppression! Down, I say!" Gesturing toward the statue of King Henri, the leader of the mob clapped his hands together. At the signal loops of rope were cast over the king's bronze head and that of his horse. Dozens of the rioters seized hold of the cables. "Together, now, citizens! Pull! Down with tyranny! Down, I say!"

What was that animal balancing on the man's shoulder? It looked like a cross between a monkey and a fox, but its skin was scaly, like snake's.

The straining at the ropes was accompanied by animal-like grunts and strangled cries. Jack saw many in the mob with demonically-empty eyes. Parted lips revealed teeth clenched in a grimace of mindless rage.

The bronze likeness resisted only briefly before leaning

perilously, then crashing to the paving stones of Paris. The king's crowned head broke off his body. The mob cheered, taking turns kicking the fallen face and the decapitated body. They clapped their hands, tossed their mob caps in the air, and pounded each others' shoulders in celebration of their bravery and their accomplishment. "Onward!" the leader commanded. "Follow me!"

The crowd roared its agreement and surged away.

"What? What was that?" Jack demanded of Eliyahu.

"King Henri worked for the good of France," Eliyahu commented. "He improved education and the lives of the common people. Mostly he was honored for his spirit of religious toleration—for encouraging Catholics and Protestants to live peacefully alongside each other in an age when religious wars and persecution were the standard."

"But—why? If he was so good, why does the mob hate him?"

"They don't really even know anything about him," Eliyahu commented. "King Henri lived almost two hundred years before the Revolution. He was assassinated on May 14, in the year 1610, by a religious fanatic. But good or bad makes no difference to the mob. They want only violence and destruction. They are also anti-God, anti-faith, and opposed to any notion that their souls will be examined by any power higher than their own. Jack—this is not only the past—this is also the future."

"And you're going to tell me that everything means something, right? I said, right, Eliyahu?"

The reproduction of Henri's statue was back on the plinth. The bridges over the Seine were again in their proper places.

Jogging slowly at first, and then faster as if to outrun the vision, Jack directed his steps back toward the canal barge and Bette.

✦ ✦ ✦

Jack guided Bette toward the Île Saint-Louis, the smaller of the two river islands that formed the heart of Paris. If the towers of Notre Dame cathedral had been smokestacks, then Île Saint-Louis was being towed behind the Île de la Cité as both steamed downriver.

"Berthillon," Jack remarked. "I've been looking forward to this. Most famous ice cream in the world, maybe. Raspberry—how do you say it in French?"

"*Framboise*" Bette instructed.

"That's it," Jack agreed. "Two giant scoops for me. How about you, Bette?"

Standing on the sidewalk, frozen treats in hand, Jack was confronted with an unusual sight: "There must be a reen-actment happening," Jack surmised. The advancing figure who caused this remark was dressed in green knee-britches, a baggy, rough-textured shirt under a green waistcoat, and was wearing a cocked hat.

Jack studied the man, who seemed to be looking around for an address. Taking another bite of *framboise* ice cream before continuing, Jack remarked, "I think he's lost. What do you think, Bette? Bette?"

She was not there. Jack was still seated at a round table. The Seine still flowed past the island. The towers of Notre Dame still loomed downstream—but the cobblestoned street was now thick with dirt.

As Jack watched, a couple dressed similarly to the first man, only in finer, newer clothes, turned the corner and approached him. "Pardon, madame, monsieur," the new-comer remarked. "Can you…."

The astonishment on Jack's face mirrored that of the questioner as the couple hurriedly drew aside, increased their pace, and strode quickly away, with many backwards glances. It took a moment for the lost individual to recover, but he tapped on the lower panel of a half-door across the street.

A man with porcine features, wearing a butcher's blood-stained apron tucked up under his armpits, and sporting a mob cap, emerged. Scowling, he demanded, "Well, citizen? What do you want?"

"Your pardon, monsieur."

Was the sound that emerged from the butcher actually a low growl? It seemed so to Jack.

"My name is Paul Daubin," the stranger said, ignoring the rude noise. "I fear I am lost. Can you help me? My son, Daniel, came to Paris for university, but I have not heard from him in some months—not since November, in fact."

"You mean, *Brumaire*, don't you, citizen?" corrected the butcher sternly. "We no longer use the old, tyrannical names for the months of the year."

"Of course, of course," Paul Daubin agreed. "At any rate, I seem to have lost my way. I thought this was the *Rue Saint Louis*, but the sign is missing…."

"Of course it's missing," the butcher bellowed. "This is *Rue de la Liberté!* Everyone knows that! Where did you say you were from, citizen?" demanded the butcher suspiciously.

"Saint-Nazaire, by the sea."

"Port Nazaire," the butcher returned. "Clothilde!" he bellowed again. "Come out here! I think this fellow is a counter-revolutionary. He still uses saints' names, and did not call me 'citizen.'"

Wiping her hands on a greasy towel, then using it to wipe her face, the butcher's wife also appeared from the shop.

"Where did you say your son lives?" Chloe narrowed her eyes and raised one eyebrow.

"On the Street of the Holy Virgin Martyrs," Paul replied. "Or so Father Lambert wrote me."

"Hold him!" Chloe shrieked.

The butcher seized Paul around the chest and shoulders.

"Hold him while I summon the Committee of Public Education," Chloe added, lunging toward a nearby doorway. "Citizen Fouche! We have caught a counter-revolutionary. Citizen! Come quickly!"

106

For just a moment—less than the blink of an eye, really—a second face appeared alongside the butcher's visage. Proud looking, the pig-like snout and squinted eyes offered a voiceless smirk, and nodded approval—before merging with the butcher's own countenance.

"But sir—madame—citizens!" Paul protested, struggling in the butcher's brawny grasp. "What have I done?"

"Consorting with the outlawed clergy! Corresponding with traitors! And if your son told anyone he lived on the Street of the Holy Virgin Martyrs, then he is a counter-revolutionary too! Everyone knows it is the *Rue Voltaire!* Citizens! Help me tie him up until—off to the gendarmerie with him."

Jack shivered, and it was not a chilling effect due the ice cream.

"Remember…." Eliyahu's voice whispered in Jack's ear. "What is past is also future…."

------------------ ✡ ✡ ✡ ------------------

Jack shook off the disturbing vision as he and Bette approached one of the most recognizable churches in the world. The twin towers of Notre Dame cathedral—Our Lady of Paris—loomed over the statue of the Emperor Charlemagne. The portrayal of the first Holy Roman Emperor, riding with upraised staff, seemed purposed to lead the eight-hundred-year ancient church into a glorious future.

Two things were misleading with this conclusion. The first erroneous note was that the statue had been completed in the late 1800s—a millennium after Charlemagne was crowned and hundreds of years after the cathedral was built.

"But if he *had* stood there in the 1790s," Jack observed, "his monument would have been torn down, both for his being a monarch and for his being a Christian. He was even called 'Blessed Charlemagne.'"

"And the other problem?" Bette queried.

Jack waved at the scaffolding still enveloping a portion of the edifice. "Because it's still not clear if Notre Dame can survive the 2019 fire damage. Some of the limestone got heated enough to crumble and a lot of it soaked up the water used to quench the fire. Since part of the roof collapsed, taking the weight off the walls makes them want to collapse inward."

"Can we go in at all?"

"No," Jack said glumly. "Besides all the danger of things falling, the lead that lined the roof melted, and some of it even vaporized. Artisans working to restore the interior have to wear breathing gear and hazmat suits—and even then they are allowed only a couple of hours exposure at a time."

"How disappointing!" Bette said.

"But just sitting out here—with you—is special," Jack said, caressing Bette's hand as they took advantage of a vacant bench.

Bette silently contemplated the towers for a time before speaking. "Do you know what I'm thinking?" she asked at last.

"Expecting Quasimodo to appear in one of the towers?" Jack teased.

Bette swatted his wrist. "No, silly. I was thinking about eight hundred years of prayers going up in this place. It puts me in mind of the Western Wall in Jerusalem."

"And yet there weren't always prayers to the Almighty delivered at his place," Eliyahu's voice commented from the side away from Bette.

Plaza, equestrian statue, bench, and Bette all vanished with a blink.

Jack found himself standing outside the cathedral—no fire damage was visible—and yet it was different. It had been vandalized. Over the doors was carved the phrase, "To Philosophy."

All the statues of the church's west façade had been decapitated. "They were the kings of Judah," Eliyahu instructed, "not French kings at all. But since they represented both monarchy and religion—they had to go. Busts of French philosophers—portraits of the so-called Enlightenment leaders—will be venerated in their place. Let's go inside."

The cavernous space was packed with people, but to describe them as worshippers was repugnant in Jack's mind. The people hooted and called out ribald suggestions as a row of seductively-clad maidens in short, white togas, swayed across the stage that replaced the sanctuary space.

"It is November 10, 1793," Eliyahu said. "Or in revolutionary practice, the twentieth of *Brumaire*. This is a new national holiday called *Fête de la Raison*—the Feast of Reason."

A flame burned atop an altar. Looming prominently over the scene was the theatrical depiction of a mountain peak. Atop it was a half-dressed woman wearing a gilt crown and holding a scepter. Behind her lurked a shadow Jack saw was capable of moving opposite to the light cast by the flames.

"The Goddess of Reason," Eliyahu noted. "Watch."

At a gesture from the woman, first the front row, and then succeeding rows of on-lookers bent on their knees, until the entire throng offered their obedience and allegiance.

"Worshipping," Eliyahu commented. "This Cult of Reason expands throughout France, as churches are desecrated and recommitted to 'Reason.'"

Around the necks and shoulders of the worshippers imps resembling the Notre Dame gargoyles slithered. Whenever the creatures paused in their crawling they crouched and whispered to the nodding heads of the followers of Reason.

"De-christianization is the order of the day," Eliyahu continued. "Atheism is enthroned in Revolutionary France. Pay attention, Jack. Atheism is *always* enthroned when

believers stop standing up and speaking up for the Truth.
Do you remember the motto of the Revolution, Jack?"

"Liberty, Fraternity, Equality?"

"Beware when mob leaders proclaim that their right
to liberty tramples the rights of other," Eliyahu warned.
"Beware when people who say they support tolerance are
the most intolerant. Beware when to curry popular acclaim
leaders say there is no need for God. Beware, Jack. What is
past is still present."

"You mean, 'what is past is future,' don't you?"
Jack inquired.

"What did *you* say, darling?" Bette said, calling Jack out
of the vision. "*I* said the breeze off the river must be making you chilly."

"Yes," Jack agreed. "I think we should go now."

✡ ✡ ✡

Jack wasn't sure it was proper—or safe—to get Eliyahu to
appear for a specific request. Jack had experienced visions
throughout Israel, and in London, and now in Paris, but
it had always been Eliyahu who initiated conversations.
Even though the arrival of the prophet no longer star-
tled or frightened him, Jack had a reluctance to ask for
him directly—it was too much like using a Ouija board or
something.

Wasn't there some prohibition against summon-
ing spirits?

Jack had little knowledge of the supernatural—and he grimaced inwardly as that thought jarred against his having witnessed dramatic events in 1948, and in the Second Century BC and now in 1790's Paris, France. What Jack was certain of was that the spirit world was nothing to mess around with.

His pondering gave way to prayer: *Lord,* Jack implored. *You have allowed me to see things and to know things that I had no human capacity to experience. I don't understand why this has been so—or why it continues—but: Jesus, I trust in You. Therefore, Jesus, if it is in Your will for me to get my questions answered at this time....*

Before the request was fully formed, the answer was already provided. "Go ahead and ask, Jack," Eliyahu agreed.

No vision this time, but the calm, cheerful voice was enough.

"At the statue of King Henry—and then again beside the ice cream shop—and also at Notre Dame—I—I saw things. It was like a vision within a vision. Like I was seeing things that the others in the vision could not see. These things, they were like living gargoyles. They were like...."

"Go ahead and use the word you are trying to avoid," Eliyahu offered.

"Demons? Was I seeing evil spirits influence humans to become even more wicked? But what—how?"

"You know what Saint Paul wrote to the Ephesians? 'For we do not wrestle against flesh and blood, but against principalities, against powers, against the rulers of the darkness of this age, against spiritual hosts of wickedness in the heavenly places...."

"So what I saw were not just—I dunno—pictures of warped souls? Those were real creatures?"

"As real as hell," Eliyahu concurred. "When the Lord Jesus delivered the possessed man in Gadara—were those demons real?"

"I—Yes," Jack responded.

"And you believe what the sacred Word says, when it records the Lord freed Mary of Magdala from seven demons?"

"Not just mental illness, was it?"

"No, Jack. Real, malevolent creatures. Do you remember being on Mount Hermon? What you witnessed there?"

"Yes," Jack drawled slowly as the images from that experience clicked into place. "I saw Satan tempting the Lord Jesus—offering Him all the kingdoms of the world—if Jesus would bow down and worship Satan."

"So if the old serpent even spoke in that way to the Lord of All Creation," Eliyahu gently urged, "do you think any of us escape from his suggestions? We are in the midst of spiritual warfare, Jack."

"Then why haven't I seen these creatures before this?"

"Does it occur to you that perhaps you weren't ready before now? That you might have questioned the truth of everything you were seeing, or been afraid to see more?"

As if Eliyahu was visibly sitting right beside him, Jack nodded his agreement. "Does that mean—I will be seeing

even more—like these? What if I really am afraid, after all?
Those are hideous things."

"What do you say, Jack? What is the motto in
your prayer?"

"Jesus, I trust in You?"

"Just so, Jack—Just so."

✧ ✧ ✧

At the eastern end of the Champs-Éllysées, Jack and Bette
strolled hand-in-hand as they approached the fountains of
the Place de la Concorde. It had rained overnight and the
streets were still damp. The air was fresh and clean, and a
north wind caused the spray of the fountains to replenish
the moisture underfoot.

"The obelisk?" Bette said, pointing at a tall spire at the
focus of the city square. "Egyptian?"

"Um-hmm," Jack agreed, consulting a guidebook.
Reading, he quoted, "Over three thousand years old. Given
to France by Egypt in 1829, it is seventy-five feet tall and
weighs two hundred eighty tons."

Bette frowned. "In kilos, please?"

Now it was Jack's turn to frown as he tried to do the
multiplication in his head. "It's…." Shaking his head and
shrugging, he replied, "A lot." Then, attempting to redeem
himself he resumed, "'It once marked the entrance to the
Luxor Temple, and celebrates the reign of Pharaoh Ramesses
the Second.' Hey! Isn't he the Pharaoh of the Ten Plagues?"

Bette nodded, then added, "In the Torah according to Cecil B. DeMille, anyway!"

Jack bobbed his head and grinned. Lifting the guidebook to eye level he prepared to continue reading. Finding the paragraph again, he read, "During the time of the French Revolution, the Place de la Concorde was called the Place de la Révolution. The spot where the obelisk now stands was occupied by—was occupied by...."

"Jack?" Bette asked. "Are you alright? Jack?"

Her voice receded in Jack's hearing as if he had suddenly moved very far away from her.

In Jack's view, the stone tower had been replaced by a wooden platform, on top of which stood a guillotine.

Shuddering, Jack lifted his right foot to back away from the execution device. The sole of his shoe squelched. The mortar between the cobblestones was thick with congealed blood.

The clean, fragrant air had been replaced by the metallic stench of blood and death.

Suddenly Jack was surrounded by a boisterous, cheering throng. A pair of Parisians mounted the platform; acting as cheerleaders for the mob. Jack saw with revulsion that the pair were the butcher and his wife from the Île Saint-Louis.

"Citizens!" Clothilde shouted. "They are coming now! Look where the enemies of the revolution are coming to meet their fate!"

A loud, mocking cheer greeted these words.

The groaning squawk of ungreased cartwheels reached

Jack's ears as the tumbril carrying the prisoners arrived beside the scaffold.

A man in uniform mounted the steps and gestured for silence. "Citizens! I am Deputy Fouche, formerly of the Committee of Public Education and now part of the Committee of Public Safety."

The throng cheered and applauded at the sight of three crouching men, dressed in rags, gaunt and obviously starving, being drawn toward their death.

"Only three?" someone in the crowd shouted. "Where are the others?"

"Yes! Why only three?"

"We were expecting dozens!"

Deputy Fouche made a placating gesture to the crowd. "Calm yourselves, citizens. I promise you that the Committee of Public Safety is ever vigilant against traitors and spies! But these are significant counter-revolutionaries—and they were captured by myself with the aid of these two worthy citizens standing here with me."

At this announcement the raucous crowd cheered again.

"Stand up, prisoners," Fouche ordered. "Citizen Cohen, stand up."

The face of the stoop-shouldered, elderly man was streaked with dried blood where chunks of his beard had been yanked out. He stood with difficulty, swaying against the loose frame of the cart.

"Citizen Cohen, you are a Jew! You were ordered out of Paris by the Committee of Public Safety, yet you returned."

"It was only to rescue a commentary by Rashi," Cohen replied in a feeble, barely audible voice. "Rashi. Hundreds of years old."

"Condemned out of your own mouth!" Fouche exulted. "Works of religion are banned."

"Guilty, guilty, guilty," chanted the crowd. "Death, death, death!"

Fouche silenced them again. "Citizen Lambert, stand up. You are condemned as a priest of the counter-revolutionary church. You also were in possession of forbidden works of superstition."

"My prayer book and a Bible," Lambert admitted.

The crowd laughed and again chorused, "Guilty, guilty!"

"And you are also guilty of harboring fugitives. One Daniel Daubin, a spy for the English."

"My son!" exclaimed the third occupant of the death-cart.

Jack was stricken. Amid the tangled hair and hunger-ravaged features of the last prisoner he finally recognized Paul Daubin whom he had seen captured on the Île Saint-Louis.

"Yes, your son," Fouche exclaimed triumphantly. "A shame he died in prison, otherwise a pair of father-and-son traitors would both pay the penalty of their crimes today!" Shrugging, the deputy enforcer said, "But the father will go to join his son today, citizens."

Amid the celebratory tumult that greeted these words, Fouche shouted, "And express your approval to this noble citizen butcher and his worthy wife! They must receive credit for helping purge the revolution of its enemies."

117

The mob cheered even louder.

The prisoners were forced to mount the scaffold, then the basket to receive their severed heads was placed in position beside the instrument of death.

"Eliyahu!" Jack pleaded. "Get me out of here! I don't want to see any more. Please!"

"Three hundred thousand arrested for speaking against the revolution," Eliyahu's voice whispered as the scene began to waver and fade. "Seventeen thousand executed and another ten thousand died in prison. Christians and others guilty of nothing more than having an opinion contrary to the mob, and of using 'hateful speech.' Past and future, Jack. Past and future."

The image of the guillotine blinked out, to be replaced by the Egyptian obelisk.

Jack found, to his surprise, he was seated on a bench. Bette sat beside him, patting his hand. "Jack! Jack!" she said urgently. "You're so pale! Are you alright?"

"I will be," Jack managed to say. "Just—just give me a minute, okay?"

6

RUE DE LA HUCHETTE

Jack showered while Bette dashed out to fetch fresh, warm baguettes, butter, coffee, a dozen eggs, cheese and mushrooms. As he shaved and dressed, the aroma of coffee and fresh omelets filled the interior of the barge. The walls were varnished golden pine. Teak floors were original to the craft and worn smooth from a hundred years of use.

The matching pine plank table in the main salon was set with royal blue ceramic plates and a vase of sunflowers. Sunlight streamed through the open skylight and beamed down on her in an ethereal light. Breathless at the sight of her, Jack stood grinning in the center of the room.

"So. Breakfast." Bette filled his mug with coffee.

"It's almost noon," he observed laughing.

"What is the old saying? When in Rome, do as the

Romans?" She served the omelets and tapped his chair, indicating where he should sit.

"Parisians call lunch, breakfast."

"Whatever. Paris. Rome. Jerusalem. As long as we are together. I have discovered I don't like clocks. And I like sharing a small bed."

"On a boat we call it a berth. And the bathroom is called the head."

"I suppose I shall have to learn these nautical terms while we are here. You are the Captain of the Ship."

"And you are First Mate."

Jack had enjoyed watching the worries of her daily life in Israel melt away. Her eyes twinkled with joy as Bette sipped strong coffee, and drank in their playful banter.

"I have decided I want to stay here with you forever. I want to share a very narrow bunk with you, so that when you turn I turn with you. I want to sleep in every morning and stay up past midnight. I want to eat warm baguettes and omelets for lunch. Maybe we should never go back to the real world, Jack. No cell phones. Only stay here."

Fresh butter on the bread melted in his mouth. "My grandmother told me stories of her life here with my grandfather before the war. Beautiful. She had an expression like I see on your face now."

"Tell me. Did she tell you places they went together?"

"Yes. Paris never changes, she said. Only the generations change, but Paris is always the same. She never came back though after the war. She said she was afraid she would see my grandfather everywhere and it would be too painful without him."

"I can understand. I never want to live without you."

"Let's not."

"It's a deal." Bette and Jack shook on it.

"They lived very near here. We can walk a bit."

"Yes, please. Show me Dodi's memories. After we wash the dishes, eh?"

✡ ✡ ✡

Rue de la Huchette ran parallel to, and existed one block inland from, the Seine. It extended about half the length of the nearby Île de la Cité. La Huchette was a short, bustling, narrow street of shops, restaurants, and night clubs.

As Bette and Jack strolled hand-in-hand along its crowded span, Jack was struck by the clamor. The buildings, though nowhere more than five stories tall, were only separated by twenty feet or so. More like an alley than a Parisian boulevard, the tops of the four-hundred-year-old structures leaned toward each other, overhanging La Huchette; threatening to collapse if the volume of noise did not hold them up.

Bette tugged Jack's arm beside a shop window displaying hats: red hats, gray hats, Panama straw hats, black woolen berets. "Jack," Bette exclaimed. "I need a beret. I must have a beret, don't you think?"

Their debate about headgear was disrupted by the

appearance of a waiter from the Greek restaurant named Brasserie Athenee next door to the *chapeau* establishment. Though it was early afternoon, the waiter wore black tuxedo trousers. The white shirt beneath the black waistcoat gleamed to match the spotless white apron he wore. With a nod in their direction, the waiter spun the plate in his hands in a display of pristine china and manual dexterity. Then, abruptly, he tossed the plate upwards, caught it on the descent, then with an intense fling of his extended arm, shattered the china on the cobblestones.

Bette, whose attention had been divided between the juggling act and the selection of hats, jumped as if a grenade had exploded, and started to draw a non-existent sidearm. Jack said soothingly, "It's okay, babe. Part of the advertising."

"Mesdames and messieurs!" the waiter commanded. "I direct your attention to Brasserie Athenee. Moussaka! Dolmadakia! And our bakhlava…." The waiter paused to kiss his fingertips. "It is to die for! Come in! Come in!"

"Bette," Jack urged. "Let's go. Coffee and pastry at least!"

Bette nodded dubiously, and as Jack started to lead her to the entrance she yanked him to a sudden halt. Her eyes narrowed, she demanded, "Why didn't *you* jump when the plate—exploded? Why were you so calm?"

Sheepishly, Jack produced the Paris guidebook from under his arm. "I was expecting it," he admitted. "Which you weren't. Wow, I'm sorry."

"Just for that," Bette said, "No pastry for you!" Then, smiling to show she wasn't really angry, she added, "Until later, anyway. We came here for you to show me the place Dodi told you about."

Number Five, Rue de la Huchette, was at the far eastern end of the street. The premises, Jack warned Bette, were now occupied by a jazz club; had been that way since just after the Second World War. "Count Basie played here," Jack said. "Lionel Hampton. Lots of famous musicians. But that's not why I want to see it. I—I'm on a pilgrimage, kind of. For Dodi, since she can't...."

Jack's words trailed away. Bette squeezed his hand as both recalled how much Jack's grandmother had aged in the last year. It was almost as if now that grandmother and grandson had been reunited, and Bette and Jack were married, and Jack had learned his Jewish heritage, and found his lord, Yeshua, that Dodi's life missions were all accomplished.

"Let's look down the passageway," Bette urged.

The entry to the courtyard of Number Five was even narrower than the La Huchette itself, and the passage twisted and turned until the way forward was blocked by a gate. "Underneath are caverns—a kind of labyrinth," Jack reported. "But the house behind the gate was the orphanage run by American sisters Rose and Betsy Smith."

Jack contemplated the house. What a life Dodi had led: from wartime Paris, to fighting for the survival of the infant state of Israel, to watching the American blessing bestowed on the Jewish nation with the moving of the U.S. Embassy to Jerusalem.

The brilliantly blue Parisian sky was suddenly overshadowed with dark gray. A spattering of rain began to fall. In the courtyard, previously empty, scores of bed sheets and diapers and shirts and nightshirts hung from countless clotheslines. A burly woman emerged from a second floor doorway, carrying a wicker basket. Over her shoulder she bellowed with a ship captain's voice of command: "Betsy! It's starting to rain! Send Claude and Rupert and Sally to help me take in the laundry!"

From behind Jack's right shoulder came the rattle of something bumping over the cobblestones. A young woman pushed a pram with difficulty, steering around the larger blocks, while resignedly controlling the bouncing baby carriage. The thin, complaining squawk of a restless infant came from beneath the hood.

In the youthful features of the mother Jack recognized Dodi. And so the baby in the pram must be....

"My mother," Jack breathed.

This was no prophetic vision; no Eliyahu-accompanied history lesson. This was purely personal.

Beside the gate hung a bell with a long chain. As Jack watched, Dodi grasped the bell-pull, then released it. Bending forward, she stooped to peer at the child. "I have to do this," Jack heard Dodi murmur. "It's because I love you so much, that I *have* to do this."

Her back stiffening with a resolve Jack had personally

witnessed, Dodi grabbed the chain and without further hesitation rang the bell. She waited only a moment for a response because the woman directing the collection of laundry turned immediately.

Jack had never before beheld forearms on a woman like these. She seemed the embodiment of Popeye the Sailor—but her voice was tender and compassionate as she opened the gate.

"Madame Rose?" Dodi inquired.

"Yes, my dear. We were expecting you. So glad you arrived before it came on to rain."

"I—I must do this," Dodi repeated as much to herself as for Rose's benefit.

"I completely understand," Rose responded sympathetically. "You are not the first mother to make such a difficult decision in these perilous times. I promise you, the child will be well looked after. You have written addresses and names down for me?"

"Yes, of course," Dodi replied, reaching into a black purse and handing over a small notebook. Shaking from shoulders to knees, Dodi started to pick up the baby, but stopped as if afraid of dropping her—or of changing her mind.

"Will you come in and have tea?" Rose said kindly. "Meet my sister and some of the other children?"

"No, I—I can't" Dodi replied. "Tell her I love her," she insisted. "I will always love her."

"I promise," Rose agreed solemnly.

As Dodi vanished into the gray mists of Paris, the World

War Two scene also disappeared, and Jack once again stood in front of an empty courtyard.

"So brave," Jack whispered to Bette. "Dodi. Saved my mother—and by that excruciating sacrifice—saved me."

"The power of one life," Bette agreed, tightly hugging Jack's arm. "God grant us that sort of bravery, even if we can't see the difference it will make."

✡ ✡ ✡

Sun shone on the tops of towering cumulus clouds, creating a dramatic backdrop of light and shadow for the bell towers of Notre Dame Cathedral.

Musicians played outside Sainte-Chapelle, promoting tickets for an evening concert of Vivaldi. The music would be held inside the jewel-like interior of the sanctuary built by King Louis IX to house the Crown of Thorns.

Street performers drew small crowds as they juggled or did comedy acts for spare change. Bette wanted to stop and watch them all in turn.

"It's a short walk back to Berthillon to buy more ice cream," Jack told her as she slowed and stopped in front of a mime on a unicycle. "And I'm running out of coins."

Bette told the mime, "We'll stop on the way back."

Suddenly the performer rocketed off his unicycle and rushed toward Jack, leaping into his arms. "Papa!" the no longer voiceless mime cried as Jack caught him.

The semi-circle of spectators roared with laughter at the

expression of surprise on Jack's face. Encouraged by the crowd the nimble performer kissed Jack on both cheeks and pleaded, "Call home, Papa! The house is on fire and the children need you!" Then he added in a hoarse whisper: "You understand, Monsieur?"

Jack dropped the messenger and stepped back. Grabbing Bette's hand he tugged her away from the scene.

She glanced at his serious expression as they hurried toward Notre Dame. "What is it, Jack?" she asked.

He shook his head. "Not now."

Bette pressed her lips tightly together and glanced around the crowds. Were they being watched? "You'll need your cell phone after all," she concluded sorrowfully.

✧ ✧ ✧

The Embassy of Israel in France was located just walking distance from the River Seine at Number Three, Rue Rabelais. It looked more like a French hotel than an official government building.

Aware that they may have been followed, Jack and Bette stopped for lunch at Le Laurent, then slipped out the back way.

A few blocks on, they spotted the blue and white flag of the State of Israel waving proudly above the entry point.

Jack presented passports and the contact information he had been given in Jerusalem.

In Hebrew, Bette gave the guards their names. After

a quick verification of papers and a phone call they were passed through the security check within minutes. Large portraits of Israeli heroes, like first president, David ben Gurion, decorated the foyer.

"It seems we are expected," Bette remarked as a uniformed IDF officer led them into the interior office wing of the building.

Bette made small talk with the officer as the secretary buzzed them into the oak paneled office of David Wise. He was a broad-shouldered, iron-jawed man with salt and pepper hair, a trim goatee, and black-framed glasses. Jack guessed he was in his mid forties.

Wise stood and extended his hand. He said, in English, with a perfect American accent, "Shalom! Jack Garrison. And Bette—now also Garrison! Congratulations are in order, I hear. Mazel Tov on your marriage!" He wore a class ring from Annapolis. An American transplant.

Jack responded pleasantly. "Yes. We're here on our honeymoon. But you know that."

Wise laughed. "Sure. We're looking after you."

Bette rubbed her cheek. "Really," she remarked flatly. "On our honeymoon."

Jack shrugged and said quietly to Bette as if Wise was not in the room, "I should have taken you to Samoa, I guess. But the quarantine lifted in Paris and, well, Samoa seemed so very far away."

Wise cleared his throat. "Look, we apologize for this interruption."

Bette and Jack sat in stony silence.

"Yes? And?" Jack said.

Wise continued. "Something has come up. In the States."

"There's a lot going on in the States. Your message to me was that the house is on fire and Papa needs me?"

Wise pushed a button and ordered coffee for all. He looked up. "Yes. Look. The whole world is on fire. Not spontaneous violence. Very well organized. And there's someone you know in L.A. Tabitha Vanderhorst? You met with her at your grandmother's house."

"You guys know too much." Jack frowned.

"We know enough to keep your grandmother safe. And you. Both of you, safe. But now we hope you will take your honeymoon on the West Coast. Simply put, we need you to meet again with Tabitha Vanderhorst. Prominent American journalist. She has reached out to Israel. Not to American authorities. I don't blame her. Who knows who can be trusted? She asked to meet with you both specifi-cally. We don't know exactly what she wants, but she made it clear she trusts you."

"That's it?" Bette asked.

Wise removed a fat envelope from his desk. "You're on your honeymoon. Who would suspect? First class air. A suite at the Beverly Wilshire."

"The pandemic. The lockdown."

"Taken care of."

"No quarantine for us, coming from Europe?"

"You meet with her. She's an old friend, after all."

Jack laughed. "We've met twice."

Wise lowered his chin. His smile faded. "She's an old friend. This is bigger than you know. If I told you that perhaps the survival of America as we know it is at stake? The survival of freedom?"

Jack felt a sudden heaviness. "Well, then. What can we say?"

Wise pushed the envelope across his desk and tapped it with his forefinger. "Say you'll continue to enjoy your honeymoon—only now in California. And so it's not too inconsiderate of us, or too exhausting for you, why not stop over in New York for a day? Take in a show? We pick up the expense."

7

FROM THE OLD WORLD TO THE NEW

Given the familiar sleep-inducing isolation of long plane flights, Jack was not surprised to fall asleep, nor surprised to find himself dreaming. *From Europe to America,* he commented to himself in his thoughts. *From the Old World to the New.*

The floor under Jack's feet rocked gently from side-to-side as the modern airliner cabin's fittings were replaced with wooden beams. The dank air was full of the sounds of creaking and groaning timbers. Jack's view was over a young man's shoulder. In a cramped, curtained space, scarcely large enough to be a cupboard, let alone a cabin, the unknown figure scribbled notes on a bound volume of blank pages—evidently a journal.

"Even though the voyage has not yet begun," Jack read, "I feel compelled to begin recording my thoughts. I am, perhaps, unreasonably hopeful. I am trusting that He who has always led our people, continues to do so in this quest for freedom to live and worship."

Who was this, and where are they bound? Jack mused. *The words are recorded in Spanish, but the sentiments were—Jewish?*

"Capitán Cristóbal Colón—already some of the men call him 'Admiral'—says we must expect a long, difficult, dangerous voyage. But I am prepared to be like Joshua—like Caleb. I will not return an evil report! I will not condemn my people to wander in the wilderness, if I can help it. The Indies or even China may be a new Promised Land after three quarters of a century of exile. What we need is a refuge where we can rebuild our lives and our faith—and prepare for the ultimate return to Zion."

Cristóbal Colón...Christopher Columbus! Then Jack was seeing— no, dreaming—a vision of the first Spanish voyage to the New World.

"If my words are at some future day discovered," the scribe continued, "then I condemn myself to the horrors of the Inquisition, but I do not care! Somehow my words will ring down through the years, and others of my tribe will follow in my footsteps.

"Already all the rest of my family have left Spain and Portugal for Holland, where there is freedom for our synagogue and our rabbis, so there is no fear in me that my words might injure those I love. Perhaps we will all be reunited in the Indies; in a land free of persecution.

"As for myself, while aboard this vessel called the 'Holy Mary,' I have no apprehension at all. Admiral Columbus is a good man. He relies for advice and translation services on a distant cousin of mine. Luis de Torres is his name—but at his *bar mitzvah* he was enrolled in the Covenant as Yosef ben haLevi! (Just as I was Baruch ben Shimon before I came to be Rodrigo da Souza.)

"On this expedition there is no reminder of the evil abroad in Spain. At least six other of my fellow crew-members are *conversos* like me. There is no member of the Office of the Inquisition aboard. The lone priest with us, Father Juan Perez, is a good man, a kind man, and not an informer. If there are spies aboard—well, I will worry about that when—and if—we make it alive back to Spain!

There are Jews on Columbus' first voyage! Jack exulted. *I think I had heard that before, but now I see it. Even if Columbus didn't yet know he was about to locate the New World, America didn't just come to the notion of religious freedom in 1776 or 1607, but all the way back here in 1492! Maybe some of my own ancestors are aboard! What if I'm related to this Baruch?*

"I must work very hard to prove my worth," Baruch wrote. "I am no sailor, and Luis Torres has vouched for me, to get me my place. I am young, unmarried, and I have won-derful eyesight, and a strong back. Hopefully, it is enough!"

✡ ✡ ✡

"We have been more than three weeks out of sight of land," Jack watched Rodrigo record in his journal. "Some of the men mutter about turning back. A few talk openly of seizing the ships and returning to Spain. Such mutinous discussion stops abruptly when I appear, because they know my cousin, Luis, is one of the most loyal among the Admiral's followers. Luis told me that a pair of brothers who were pressed into service against their will may have been the deliberate cause of the rudder failure that had to be repaired early in the trip.

"Last night I overheard the Admiral in conversation with my cousin. My relation counsels against despair. He points out that the winds have been favorable this entire journey, and that we are not short of either water or provisions. He also reminded the Admiral that it was I who had spotted a flight of birds all heading in a particular direction toward the southwest, and that we had altered course to follow them.

"This the Admiral conceded, but added that another four days had already passed, and no more flocks of birds had been seen.

"How much further we can travel westward without finding land—and still have enough supplies for the return voyage—is, I think, in the mind of every crewman.

"I stood my latest watch in the darkest hours. I saw a myriad of stars, reveling in the sky's river of light, called by the prophet Daniel, *Nehar di-nur*, 'The Stream of Fire.' I heard whales rise and spout. I thought—pleasant imagining—that a wayward puff of wind brought the aroma of green plants and warm, moist earth—but likely I dreamed it. What I did not see was any sight of land.

"Another man, also called Rodrigo, replaced me in the lookout post above the mainsail. I am sorely in need of sleep, but I wanted to commit these thoughts to writing first. May *HaShem* grant this voyage has not been in vain! There must be a Promised Land at the end of fifteen centuries of journeys. There must be!"

A confused shouting and a sudden rush of stomping feet came from the deck above. Both Rodrigo's head and Jack's snapped toward the companionway, trying to decipher the cascading noise. And then a single, excited, high-pitched voice broke through the tumult: "Land! Captain! Admiral! Land, ho!"

"*Baruch atem Adonai*.... Rodrigo wrote. "Blessed art Thou, O Lord, King of the Universe, Who has allowed us to live to see this day. A new vista opens; a new chance to worship without fear. And perhaps I will be able to freely have more conversations with Father Perez about this one called Yeshua of Nazareth, King of the Jews."

✿ ✿ ✿

The cramped space of Rodrigo's berth vanished, as did the Santa Maria. What replaced it in Jack's vision was an island, solid ground after the rolling and tossing of the ship. The sun was warm underfoot, and the white sand of the beach had both the consistency and the color of refined sugar.

Jack heard Rodrigo whisper in amazement to a comrade,

"I never knew there were so many different colors of—green. And the ocean—such brilliant blue."

Rodrigo's shipmate responded, "Palm trees like on Mallorca, where I'm from. But have you ever seen flowers like these? Of course you haven't! We must be in the Indies for certain!"

In his formal dress robes of scarlet and gold, Admiral Columbus alone among the newly arrived voyagers mirrored the dramatic colors of the surrounding foliage. The captain of the Santa Maria stepped forward, holding a furled banner. Approaching Columbus, the officer cleared his throat and nodded toward the royal emblem.

"Not yet," Rodrigo and Jack overheard Columbus reply. "Something else must be done first." Dropping to his knees, Columbus gestured for all his companions to copy him.

"O Lord," Columbus prayed as he lifted his eyes toward a sky dotted thickly with fluffy, white clouds. "Eternal and Omnipotent God. Thou hast, by Thy holy word, created the heavens, the earth and the sea. Blessed and glorified be Thy name. Praised be Thy majesty, who hast deigned that, by means of Thy unworthy servant, Thy name should be acknowledged and made known in this new quarter of the world." Crossing himself fervently, the Admiral said firmly, "Amen."

Rodrigo and all the others echoed him, as did Jack, though no one heard him.

"This new quarter of the world," Jack heard Rodrigo repeat in a wondering tone. "A new quarter—a new

beginning—a place to worship without fear. What
will it mean?"

Together all the men recited the Credo: "I believe in
God, the Father Almighty, Creator of Heaven and Earth,
and in Jesus Christ, His Only Son, our Lord...."

"I'm not sure about this son of yours," Rodrigo
remarked so quietly that only Jack noticed it. "But in this
land, if You, Lord God, King of the Universe, choose to
show him to me—I am ready to learn. Omaine."

Rising from his knees and brushing off the sand, the
Admiral announced, "And I proclaim this place—San
Salvador—Holy Savior—and claim it and its inhabitants for
the sake of Our Lord Jesus Christ!"

✿ ✿ ✿

"You failed again, didn't you?" Bone Box asserted bluntly.
"An agent killed in Hebron. Another one—an important
associate—near Ariel. Now a missed opportunity in Paris."

Rahman's head hung on his chest and he spoke without
making eye contact. "It should have been so easy. Paris is
not crowded, like it usually is! It is too simple for my oper-
atives to be spotted. And then, the abrupt, unexpected
departure. We thought we had weeks to...."

"You are making excuses?"

There was no possible reply to what was manifestly true.

"Take to heart what I have told you about where
American support for Israel rests," Bone Box ordered.

"Learn what is important to us and our plans. Think more broadly."

Rahman perked up. Perhaps there was going to be a reprieve after all. "In the evangelical churches?" he answered.

"Just so. What would happen to U.S. support for the Jewish state if Americans could not freely worship; could not assemble for their pastors to urge aid to Israel? What if soft, complacent Americans were suddenly faced with persecution? What if, as a result, American support of a pro-Israel presidential administration faltered, and an election ushered in an anti-Jewish president?"

"America would abandon Israel."

"So. You see how things tie together?"

"I do," Rahman agreed fervently. "I do."

"Good," Bone Box agreed. "Then I have one more matter that must be handled. A nosy journalist who is too—shall we say—inquisitive—for her own good. Already she discovers connections and she guesses—correctly—at even more. This must not be allowed to be communicated to anyone who can disrupt my plans. I know you will be pleased to assist me with silencing her voice as well? She has even been in contact with Garrison and Deekmann. Is my meaning clear enough?"

"It shall be attended to," Rahman agreed.

8

The Almighty Keeps His Promises

Bette and Jack slept soundly in their luxurious suite in Trump Tower, New York City. It was past midnight when there came a sound like a riot in the streets. Awakened from a deep sleep, Jack knew before he opened his eyes that Eliyahu was in the room. Bette slept on, unable to hear the voice of the prophet or the other clamor.

The chants of thousands of celebrating women rose up from the broad Avenue. "It's my body! It's my choice! It's my body! It's my choice!"

"Eliyahu. I know you are here." Jack addressed the figure in the shadows. "What is left for me to see?"

"Look out the window," Eliyahu directed.

Jack rose and parted the blackout curtains. All around New York City, tall skyscrapers were lit up with shades of pink which blended into dark red at the pointed tops, giving the buildings the appearance of bloody syringes.

A mob of frenzied women danced and screamed in front of the Trump hotel. It was among the few buildings which was not illuminated in the macabre, death-like symbol.

Jack asked, "What am I seeing?"

"The past. They are celebrating evil. January 22, 2019. Almost one year to the week from when the plague would be unleashed in New York. This was night the governor of New York signed unlimited abortion into law in this state. Governor Cuomo and other political leaders gathered to sign the death warrant for tens of thousands of infants whose beating hearts and functioning organs would be harvested for profit. And the women who celebrated murdering their children in the womb shrieked, 'This is my body!'"

Jack observed with horror the wild crowd shouting at the entrance to Trump's building. Hovering above them, weaving through them, entering their bodies, and howling with glee, thousands of opaque gray, spirit-wraiths rejoiced at Satan's victory. The slaughter of innocent children was now the law.

The memory of Shakespeare's play, *Macbeth*, came vividly to Jack's mind. "Lady Macbeth," he said aloud.

"Yes," Eliyahu agreed.

"In the play, she prayed for demons to take away her woman's heart."

"Remember her words, Jack, for that is what you are seeing."

"Lady Macbeth cried, 'Come, you spirits that tend on mortal thoughts, unsex me here, and fill me from the crown to the toe; top full of direst cruelty.'"

"And so that prayer to demons has gone out from the mouths of evil since before the age of Jezebel and the sacrifice of infants to the fires of the demon god Molech."

"But why?" Jack pleaded.

"Listen to their chants. Listen to them!"

The howling voices rose up, "MY BODY! MY BODY!"

Eliyahu explained, "Abortion is the Anti-Christ's demonic parody of the Last Supper. Yeshua, broke the bread and said, 'This is my body which is broken for you.' That is why the demons distort the same holy words, 'This is my body' with the blasphemous opposite meaning."

Jack nodded, understanding Evil's mockery of holy communion. "And so here, the demons inhabit humans, and gather on the steps of the president's building. Why do they hate him so much?"

"Because of all the American presidents, Trump is the first in this generation who has stood strong for Life; for the right of children in the womb to live. His is the only voice in such an exalted office who has ever spoken out for the lives of infants. He speaks for children who have no voice. For this righteous stand, Satan hates this American president above every living human. The president has aligned himself with Life. He fights against Lucifer himself, the terrible enemy of mankind's souls. And along with this, in all Trump has accomplished, he has supported Israel.

Therefore, every demon has turned its focus on destroying the ancient, holy mandate of restoration and life. The
Cyrus Mandate. If ever the President lets go of his mandate, great calamity will come to these shores."

"You have shown me the past, and yet the past is on
going in the present. What does the future hold?"

"You have seen what was. It is connected to what is.
Soon I will show you the future of what is to come upon
this place unless the people turn from their evil ways and
repent. But for now there is more of the past to visit and
explore. More spiritual heritage in danger of being lost.
Come with me."

✡ ✡ ✡

Jack recognized the scene from history playing out before him
and Eliyahu. The sailing ships *Susan Constant, Godspeed* and
Discovery rested serenely at anchor off the coast of Virginia.

Jack and Eliyahu had stepped from the clamor of a vast
modern port city into the Jamestown story of 1607. They
stepped into a story Jack recognized from his earliest grade
school history books.

Over a lifetime, Jack had seen men dressed like these
portrayed in patriotic paintings, documentaries, and film.
Now here they were, living, breathing, and looking far from
heroic. They seemed to be just ordinary men.

Gentle waves lapped the shore where small boats were
dragged up onto the sand. A breeze carried the sweet scent

of the dense forest and earth. Seagulls wheeled and cried above their heads.

The English settlers of the Virginia Company gathered and discussed the site they had chosen for their new settlement.

"We should plant the flag of England," remarked a strong, young man, with broad shoulders and calloused hands like a farmer. "For King James who sent us forth on this enterprise."

Another, older fellow, shook his head in disagreement. "Not the banner first. No. Not the banner of King James. Nay, rather we shall raise the cross of Jesus Christ and claim this great land only for the King of Heaven and Earth. For this land shall first of all belong to King Jesus."

The company cheered his words. The ship's carpenter was instructed to bring the cross from the boat. Others set to digging a hole in which to plant the tree of Calvary.

The farmer added, "Aye. But we shall name our settlement after the King. King James. We shall call this settlement Jamestown."

A murmur of agreement passed through the all-male crowd. Jack noted there was not one woman among them all.

An elder doffed his hat and looked heavenward. "Aye. T'was King James who gave us the Bible which all literate men in England may read in their own tongue. So now we shall mark this day, gentlemen! Remember forever: the founding of Jamestown."

A cheer rose up as the cross was planted.

"One day perhaps our descendants will remember and celebrate the date of our beginning in the New World. On this day, May 14, in the year of our Lord, 1607."

Another huzzah arose, echoing in the forest. Those men who remained on the ships replied with a shout of jubilation across the water.

At last, Eliyahu spoke: "Jack, we have come here not only to witness the beginning of America. But it is the calendar I wish you to consider and remember, Jack. This is the date when events of great and eternal significance were first planted on the very edge of America. Even something as small as the date matters, you see? May 14, 1607."

Jack knew he had seen everything Eliyahu intended for him to see. The events unfolding from this moment of triumph would involve starvation, death, and unspeakable horrors.

But this moment, this date, was the beginning of the story.

Eliyahu raised his hand in gesture of priestly benediction over the assembly. "We have seen enough here." He raised his face and closed his eyes. "Come along now, Jack."

✧ ✧ ✧

Morning sunlight on the bell tower of the Pennsylvania State House cast a long shadow across the broad expanse of lawn where the representatives of the states gathered outside.

Eliyahu remarked to Jack, "The Congressional Custodian who keeps the keys is late. The doors of the hall are locked."

Viewing the group of men from the shadows cast by the elms framing the walkway, Jack thought it was as though a portrait of the American Founding Fathers had come to life. He spotted several prominent men milling around among the crowd: James Madison, Alexander Hamilton, and George Washington were all present, Jack noted, but Benjamin Franklin was the most easily recognizable.

"Philadelphia. A gathering of eagles," Jack remarked.

"And here comes David, the Custodian, with the key to let the flock enter for the debate which shall decide the future of America."

Great men parted for a small, elderly man wearing a flat-brimmed Quaker hat and black clothing.

"Good morrow, David," a Quaker representative whom Jack did not recognize, called to the caretaker. "Thou art late!"

"I have the key," the fellow raised his hand above his head. "Never late! Thou art all early!" The key turned, the doors swung wide, and the representatives poured into the Hall.

John Adams doffed his hat to the Custodian, "Ah, tis the key of David!" Adams recited the passage from Revelation 3. "What He opens no one can shut, and what He shuts no one can open. See, I have placed before you an open door that no one can shut."

"What is the date?" Jack asked. "And what is the significance?"

"If I tell you the date, by your calendar, you will know the rest." Eliyahu paused. "May 14, 1787."

Jack replied without hesitation. "The first day of America's Constitutional Convention. The beginning of the Hundred Day debate."

Eliyahu agreed. "Do not forget this. May 14, 1787. A date recorded in history. And recorded in heaven. Everything means something. A day of great significance, in the past, in the present, and in the future."

✡ ✡ ✡

With a broad sweep of Eliyahu's arm, Jack and the prophet suddenly sat unseen among the Jewish congregation of a synagogue. "We are in Touro synagogue in Newport, Rhode Island. It was first called, by the Hebrew name, *Yeshuat Israel.* Salvation of Israel. The year is 1790."

"Yeshuat? So close to the Hebrew name of Jesus."

"And so it is," Eliyahu agreed. "This is a moment for the Jews of America which is eternally recorded in the heavens. You see, the U.S. Constitution has been ratified. Rhode Island was the last to sign and so the last state for the President to visit.

"And there he is." Jack recognized two men in the synagogue immediately. Tall and dignified, George Washington, America's First President, stood on the dais beside a much smaller man, a Jew in a prayer shawl, who looked very much like Lev Seixas!

In amazement Jack remarked, "Eliyahu! George Washington has just stepped out of a painting. I would know him anywhere. But the fellow beside him? He looks so much like—well, almost identical to my friend Lev. It's like seeing Lev dressed up in a costume."

"The legacy is long. The heritage is clear. Yes. You see, that is the great-grandfather, back several generations, of your friend, Lev Seixas. His name is Moses Seixas. Seixas was warden here at the Newport Synagogue, and an important official among the Jewish congregations through-out the thirteen states of the new nation. Letters of cove-nant have been exchanged between Seixas and President Washington. I will show you the holy pact made between the first American president and the Jews of America. Washington has come to the Jewish house of worship for a very important reason." Eliyahu held up his finger for Jack to listen as Moses Seixas stepped to the Bema.

Seixas opened a scroll and began to read: "Sir, permit the Children of the Stock of Abraham to approach you with the most cordial affection and esteem for your person and merits—and to join with our fellow citizens in welcom-ing you to Newport.

"With pleasure we reflect on those days—those days of difficulty and danger, when the God of Israel, who delivered David from the peril of the sword—shielded your head in the day of battle. And we rejoice to think, that the same spirit who rested in the bosom of the greatly beloved Daniel, enabling him to preside over the Provinces of the Babylonish Empire, rests and will ever rest upon you, enabling you to discharge the arduous duties of Chief Magistrate in these States.

"Deprived as we heretofore have been of the invaluable rights of free citizens, we now with a deep sense of gratitude to the Almighty disposer of all events behold a government, erected by the Majesty of the People—a government, which to bigotry gives no sanction, to persecution no assistance—but generously affording to all, liberty of conscience, and immunities of citizenship. Deeming every one, of whatever nation, tongue, or language, equal parts of the great governmental machine. This so ample and extensive Federal Union whose basis is philanthropy, mutual confidence, and public virtue, we cannot but acknowledge to be the work of the Great God, who ruleth in the Armies of Heaven among the Inhabitants of the Earth, doing whatever seemeth Him good.

"For all these blessings of civil and religious liberty which we enjoy under and equal and benign administration, we desire to send up our thanks to the Ancient of Days, the great preserver of men. Beseeching him, that the angel who conducted our forefathers through the wilderness into the Promised Land, may graciously conduct you through all the difficulties and dangers of this mortal life. And when, like Joshua, full of days and full of honor, you are gathered to your Fathers, may you be admitted into the Heavenly

Paradise to partake of the water of life, and the tree of immortality.

"Done and signed by the order of the Hebrew Congregation in Newport, Rhode Island, August 17, 1790.

"Moses Seixas, Warden"

There followed a long pause and then a huge burst of applause exploded. The congregation leapt to their feet and cheered. George Washington, a broad smile on his face, accepted the scroll and offered his hand to Seixas.

Jack met the somber gaze of Eliyahu who rose and said, "And so it begins. The Jewish prayers invoking the Holy Spirit to lead the patriarchs of Israel have here called that same Spirit to anoint the first President of the United States of America, and give him a mandate like the one given to Cyrus; to protect the Jewish people." Eliyahu took Jack's arm. "Come now and see the response which followed."

Suddenly Jack and Eliyahu stood in the shadows of a man's study. The space was lit by multiple candles. A ring of light radiated out from an oil lamp. Washington sat at his writing desk. A sheet of linen stationery was before him. He held a quill which he dipped in the ink well, paused, and then began to write. The scratch of nib on the paper accompanied his whispered thoughts.

"I received with much satisfaction your Address. I rejoice in the opportunity that I shall always retain a grateful remembrance of the cordial welcome I experienced in my visit to Newport....

"We cannot fail to become a great and happy people.

The citizens of the United States of America have a right to applaud themselves for having given to mankind examples of a policy worthy of imitation...."

The great man paused and gazed upward in deep thought before he resumed writing.

"It would be inconsistent with the frankness of my character not to avow that I am pleased with your favorable opinion of my administration, and fervent wishes for my felicity. May the Children of the Stock of Abraham, who dwell in this land, continue to merit and enjoy the goodwill of the other inhabitants, while everyone shall sit in safety under his own vine and fig tree and there shall be none to make him afraid. May the Father of all mercies scatter light and not darkness in our paths, and make us all in our several vocations useful here, and in his own due time and way everlastingly happy.

"G. Washington"

The president leaned back in his chair and sighed with satisfaction. He laid down the quill and blotted the ink.

Only then did Jack notice that Washington was in his stocking feet.

Silence. Then Eliyahu remarked, "And from the beginning of the United States of America; from the first American President, the Children of the Stock of Abraham were a part of the dream of Freedom. For the first time since the Diaspora, Jews were safe in America, free from persecution. Living in a nation that gave no room for bigotry or persecution—until the time was fulfilled for the people of Israel to return home to the Land of their Fathers. America would be there for them even then."

✡ ✡ ✡

The American flag and the President's flag adorned with the Great Seal of the United States flanked Harry S. Truman's desk. Jack noted the olive branch with thirteen leaves and thirteen olives, seemed to be in the left talon of the eagle; different than in the present rendering.

Eliyahu and Jack were not in the Oval Office, but clearly this was the headquarters of the President.

A tall walnut hutch containing a radio was the focus of attention near President Harry S. Truman's desk. Truman, hands folded on the blotter, gazed steadily at the open Bible. The desk calendar displayed the date: MAY 14, 1948.

Several other government officials, none of whom Jack recognized, were seated around the office. A young man in a military uniform fiddled with the dial and checked his watch.

"Any minute now, Mr. President."

Truman nodded curtly. "For the first time in two thousand years we will hear the Children of the Stock of Abraham tell of their own nation. The nation of Israel."

Eliyahu and Jack stood near the radio. Suddenly the speaker crackled and music began to play. A distant voice spoke in Hebrew as a rabbi, seated at Truman's right, interpreted the historic announcement.

"Mr. President, David Ben Gurion is speaking now...."

Truman began to write as Ben Gurion spoke.

"I shall now read to you the founding document of the State of Israel that was approved by the People's Council....

"The Land of Israel was the birthplace of the Jewish people. Here, their spiritual, religious and political identity was shaped. Here they first attained to sovereignty, created cultural values of national and universal significance and gave unto the world The Eternal Book of Books.

"After being forcefully driven out to exile the Jewish people kept the faith throughout the time in foreign countries and never ceased to pray and hope to return to their homeland and renew their independence."

Truman quietly agreed, "I heard these very words from my Jewish friends in Missouri growing up."

Ben Gurion continued, "Out of this historical and traditional connection Jewish people in every generation sought to return to their ancient homeland. In recent times they have arrived in numbers. Pioneers and defenders flourished in the wilderness, revived the Hebrew language, built villages and towns and created a thriving community with their own economy and culture. Peace seeking, yet self-reliant, they brought progress to favor the whole land and are aspiring towards independence."

Truman spoke, "You know Mark Twain, a Missouri native himself, wrote about the curse that was over that land until the Jews began to return. He said if a fly was on your horse when you rode down to the sea from Jerusalem, you knew the fly came from Jerusalem because there was no life anywhere else."

The rabbi smiled. "True. True."

Truman fell silent as Ben Gurion spoke again. "In the year 5657 Jewish calendar, 1897, the first Jewish Congress had gathered to the call of the visionary Theodor Hertzl, and declared the right of the Jewish people to a national rebirth in their own State. This right was recognized in the Balfour Declaration given on the second of November, 1917, and reaffirmed with the Mandate of the League of Nations, which in particular gave international statute to the historic connection between the Jewish people to the Land of Israel and to the right of the Jewish People to re-establish their national home.

"The holocaust which recently befell the Jewish people in which millions were massacred in Europe, proved again the necessity of the Jewish people to have an independent homeland. Renewing the Jewish State in the Land of Israel will open the gates of the homeland for every Jewish Person and give unto the Jewish people the status of an Equal Nation within the family of nations."

Truman agreed, "You wonder how many Jewish lives would have been saved it there was a Jewish Homeland before the Nazis."

As if in reply, Ben Gurion said, "Survivors of the Nazi carnage in Europe and Jews of other countries contin-ued to arrive to the Land of Israel. In spite of difficulties, restrictions, and dangers, they never ceased to assert their

right to live a life of dignity, freedom and honest toil in their
national homeland. In the Second World War the Hebrew
Community of this land contributed its full share in the
struggle of freedom and peace-keeping nations against the
evil Nazi forces. And the blood of its troops and its war
effort gained the right to belong among the founders of the
United Nations. On the 29th of November, 1947, the UN
General Assembly adopted the resolution 181 which requires
the founding of a Jewish State. The General Assembly
demands the residents of the land to take this positive step
towards the implementation of that resolution. The recognition by the UN of the right of the Jewish people their State
is irrevocable. It is the natural right of the Jewish people to
be as any other nation, self-reliant in their own sovereign
state. Therefore we gathered, we, members of the People's
Council, Representatives of the Hebrew Community and
the Zionist Movement, on the day the British Mandate
over the land ends, by the virtue of our natural and historic
right and based upon the UN resolution, we hereby declare
the establishment of the Jewish State in the Land of Israel.
Which would be called: The State of Israel.

"We declare open for Jewish migration, Aliya, and the
ingathering of the exiles would strive to develop the land
for the good of all its residents as based on the foundations
of Liberty, Justice, and Peace as envisaged by the Prophets
of Israel."

Applauding, Truman pushed back his chair and stood.
All the room cheered, and joined him.

The translator spoke above the noise.

"We sign, May 14, 1948.

"Blessed are you, Lord, our God, King of the World, for bringing us to these times. Amen!"

Still standing, Truman passed a typed sheet of paper embossed with the Great Seal of the United States, to his assistant. "Read this for everyone to hear," he instructed.

The assistant studied the words for a moment, then began.

"This government has been informed that a Jewish State has been proclaimed in Palestine, and recognition has been requested by the provisional government thereof. The United States recognizes the provisional government as the de facto authority of the new State of Israel.

Signed: Harry S. Truman

Approved: May 14, 1948"

More applause erupted from the gathering.

Truman raised his hand for silence. "My mother taught me a Bible verse about those who bless the land and the Children of the Stock of Abraham." He picked up his Bible and thumbed to a verse. "Genesis 12:1-3. God made a covenant with Abraham. He said, 'I will bless those who bless you and curse those who curse you' I believe that promise, gentlemen, and I want America to continue to be blessed by Almighty God." He paused and turned to his assistant. "America should be the first to bless Israel. Quick! Go now, and send the wire to Ben Gurion!"

The assistant saluted and hurried out the door.

With the wave of Eliyahu's hand, the vision of Israel's national symbol appeared. A blue banner with the central image of a menorah was flanked by two olive branches.

"Count the leaves on each olive branch." Eliyahu grasped Jack's arm.

Jack counted and gasped. "Thirteen! Thirteen leaves on each branch of the Israeli flag! The Great Seal also has thirteen on its olive branch!"

Eliyahu replied with an enigmatic smile, "Twelve olives, for Israel representing the twelve tribes of Israel. But you must ask yourself in the scope of all things eternal, why the seals of both Israel and the United States of America have olive branches with thirteen olive leaves?"

"Tell me! Please, Eliyahu! Explain the connection!"

"Connection is the word, Jack. And as the people of the new nation of Israel danced in the streets, before their war for survival began, President Harry Truman and the great nation of America was indeed the first to acknowledge the rebirth of the Israel. May 14, 1948, in Washington, D.C. and in Tel Aviv, Israel, the ancient prophecy became reality. Those who bless are blessed. Remember, Jack: The Almighty keeps his promises."

The scene before Jack began to fade in a swirling mist. Jack closed his eyes and returned to a deep and tranquil sleep.

9

CLEAR AND PRESENT DANGER

"Hurry up in there," Jack called. "I'm starving."

Listening to Bette singing in the shower made a smile dance across his face. It was Sunday morning and after yet another long-distance flight, and with no business to occupy them before tomorrow, Jack intended to enjoy the Beverly Wilshire accommodations to the fullest. Room service, for sure.

Idly, Jack pressed the power button on the television remote control. Jack had never spent any time sorting out the English-language channels in Israel, so this should be a treat.

The previous occupant had left the channel set to CNN. "California Governor Newsom," the broadcaster gushed, "in a bid to once again contain the virus threat, has ordered restaurants and churches to stop holding public meetings.

Outdoor gatherings in the affected counties are still permitted for the moment."

A photo of the masked governor appeared on the screen. *Wasn't this the same guy who ruled that singing or chanting in church was not permitted?* Jack wondered.

"Schools will similarly be required to remain closed to on-campus instruction," the reporter continued. "Meanwhile, in other news, protesters continue to demonstrate for racial equality and the removal of offensive statues and monuments."

The headshot of Newsom was replaced with video of protestors marching shoulder-to-shoulder, unmasked. Roping a statue, the mob pulled it from its pedestal, while everyone cheered and applauded.

Stabbing his finger down on the remote, Jack changed the channel. His random selection produced a church service. The tall, slim, dark-haired pastor smiled at the camera. "Our mission—our number one job, if you will— is to birth goodness into the world; to give people hope; to help people feel better about themselves. That means it's your job too. Everyone of you is destined for greatness. How many of you have guilt in your lives? God didn't give you that feeling! He loves you just the way you are."

Jack listened carefully. He had an innate distrust of television preachers ever since Jack's father discovered that Jack's grandmother was sending half her monthly social security income to one of those TV preachers who always seemed to be in greater need than she herself.

Listening attentively, Jack tried to be fair.

"It doesn't matter how you were raised," the pastor continued. "It doesn't matter what you call yourself: Christian, Muslim, Jewish, or nothing at all! God is still God for everybody. Can't you feel it?"

Oh-oh, Jack thought. *Where's Jesus in all this?*

"Even though we can't physically be together right now, God still loves you. Don't worry about the things you can't do. Be positive! Keep expecting good things and good things will come to you. And if you're depressed, try not to worry about it. Jesus got weary sometimes."

When Jack exhaled he discovered he'd been holding his breath; waiting for Jesus' name to get mentioned. Perhaps the direction of this sermon would resolve into something Christian after all.

"Jesus was depressed," the pastor continued. "Once He got so down—I don't remember where this happened, but it doesn't matter—He was so depressed that blood popped out on His forehead instead of sweat. God never wanted that. He doesn't want you to suffer, either. He doesn't want you to be unhappy. It's okay to be depressed—just don't stay there. The world is too good. You have too much to live for. God wants to bless you, but you have to believe in yourself first."

Jack felt sick to his stomach.

"God wants everything to be better for you tomorrow than it is today. He wants you to have more love in your life, more success, more money, more of what makes you happy—because God wants you to be happy. Don't believe any of these doom-and-gloom folks! Just keep making the world a little better each day and it will get better for you too.

"Now I want to share with you a little about our financial needs here at this ministry. You know, you can't outgive God. We are going to need twenty-five million dollars for our television outreach. Dealing with the world according to Covid...." the pastor winked at the camera. "Good programming is more important than ever, amen?"

Snapping off the television, Jack filled a glass with ice water from the carafe on the night table and pressed it against his forehead. *No word about the evil in the world*, Jack lamented. *No word about turning from sin and turning to Jesus.*

Jack couldn't help himself. Grabbing up his smart phone he demanded information about the home church whose mega-auditorium he had just witnessed. Annual income: one hundred million dollars. Television outreach: twenty-five million dollars. Support to missionaries: one million dollars.

That's it? Jack thought. *God wants you to be happy. Tune in again next week and I'll tell you the same thing again?*

Bette emerged from the bathroom, barefoot, toweling her hair, and enveloped in a plush robe. "Breakfast?" she asked. "Pancakes? Nice, kosher omelet?"

"I dunno," Jack replied. "Maybe a glass of juice. I'm not as hungry as I thought I was."

CLEAR AND PRESENT DANGER

✿ ✿ ✿

Of the two thugs hired by Brahim Rahman, the larger was clearly the lesser in brain power. Six and a half feet tall, two hundred seventy pounds, "Tiny" was often warned not to strain his mental powers.

His partner was eight inches shorter and one hundred pounds lighter, but no less lethal. Glen was an excellent shot with his Taurus .38, but his second preference was for the thin-bladed knife hung inside his aloha shirt by a loop around his neck. Best of all he liked the wire garrote concealed within his waistband. The noose was quick, silent, and more reliable than bullet or blade.

"So, what's she done, eh?" Tiny wanted to know. "Cheated on you? Stole? I know," he said attempting to snap his fat fingers. "You want no cops. No cops must mean she's got something on you, right?"

"Tiny," Glen warned. "Shut your mouth, eh? Not our business."

Rahman's eyes narrowed. He had spent a considerable sum already locating this pair of supposedly professional killers, but so far these two were a bad comedy team. "Exactly," he warned.

"Look," Glen said soothingly. "He didn't mean nothing by it. Just show us the target and we do the rest. That is," he added, "after we see the payment."

"Ten thousand now and ten more when the job is

done," Rahman said, tossing an envelope of cash onto the chipped surface of the table in the cheapest, grungiest hotel on Ventura Boulevard.

Glen counted the bills, then nodded at Tiny. "So? Who is it?"

From the jacket pocket that recently contained the money Rahman's gloved hands produced a photograph of an attractive young blonde and flung it to the table as well.

"She gotta name?" Tiny asked.

"Tabitha Vanderhorst," Rahman replied. "Address is on the back."

"When's it to be?" Glen wanted to know.

"As soon as possible," was the response. "Rest of the payment when I read about it in the paper."

✿ ✿ ✿

Tabitha Vanderhorst, masked with a red bandana as instructed, was waiting outside Factory Tea Bar near the burned-out shell of California's San Gabriel Mission when Jack and Bette arrived. Tabitha's long blond hair, tied up in a ponytail, was threaded through the back of a navy blue ball cap with Minnie Mouse on the front.

In front of her, on the round metal table, a copy of the *Los Angeles Times* was open to pages two and three of the Sunday Arts section. Photographs of Dodi and her Jerusalem home and art gallery were displayed on the cover.

"There she is." Bette squeezed Jack's hand. It had been several weeks since they had last seen Tabitha in Israel.

From her urgent message to Jack and Bette, it was clear that Tabitha was almost certainly being followed.

"Tabitha!" Bette cried as they approached.

"Hi, Tabitha," Jack joined in enthusiastically.

Tabitha half rose, then sat again quickly. Jack guessed she was in some distress. Her pale blue eyes betrayed fear.

She remarked, "Sorry. Social distancing stuff. No hugs."

Jack lowered his voice as they sat. "And our masks mean no lip reading in case we're being filmed."

"We are being filmed." Tabitha glanced to the left.

About twenty-five feet away an olive-skinned young man in tight, ripped jeans, and a black BLM shirt pretended to be texting. His phone was pointed directly at the trio. "He's been shadowing me for a couple hours. Since I left my house."

"Are you in danger?" Jack leaned his elbow on the table.

"Maybe. Yes. You know how it's been. People who know things which can incriminate the Left are 'committing suicide' by the dozens. I wouldn't want to turn up on that list."

"And you're still a reporter for *The Times*?" Bette asked.

Tabitha nodded curtly, then replied, "I can't stay there. Dangerous. Getting more so. I know too much. I was making coffee in the break room. I heard an editor in a nearby storage room talking on her cell phone. Telling someone about the need to burn churches. The lockdown of churches wasn't effective. And they would start with the California Mission churches and also attack synagogues. She said smoke and fire would get some attention. Burning the President's Church across from the White House was almost ignored. Oh, but Trump holding up his Bible. The press spun that into a presidential photo-op, and it worked. She said the protests weren't enough. Not enough happening here in L.A. It was the West Coast's turn. This is global. Orchestrated by forces outside the U.S., but the collusion of Leftist political leaders and the media to bring down America. This is real." She paused. "Listen. There are going to be more attacks. On churches and on people. The congregations. I'm talking massacres unless churches are smart enough to get serious about security. I mean it. This is all out war against Christianity and the Constitution."

"Did she know you overheard?" Jack probed.

Tabitha winced. "She opened the door and saw me looking stupid with my cup of coffee. Thank God I was wearing my mask. She hung out in the doorway and flat out asked me if I overheard her. Was I eavesdropping? She asked what I thought about the ANTIFA protests. Tearing down Christian statues. I told her what I thought. That this had gone way too far. It wasn't about George Floyd's murder. Or racism. It was senseless, anti-American violence."

"What was her response?"

"She mocked me. She said, 'Anti-American? What's that? Spoken like a true Nazi racist.' I reminded her I'm

Jewish. That pushed her over the edge. She raged at me about ANTIFA and BLM for a full ten minutes, then stormed out."

"Then what?"

"Then San Gabriel Mission Church was burned. And the church attacks and vandalism of synagogues increased. The same week, in Manila, the Philippines, the centuries-old Church of Santo Niño went up in flames."

"Church of the Holy Infant." Jack translated.

Tabitha continued. "The names of the sites being targeted. The origins of Christianity. Think about it. I knew *The Times* editor wasn't having an idle conversation about desecration of Christian sites. I knew that she, a prominent media leader, is involved. This is a propaganda machine for the Globalists. What I overheard wasn't a coincidence."

Bette asked, "What's to be done about it?"

Tabitha frowned, "We've got to have a grass roots effort. Ordinary people are going to have to stand up, and speak out, and resist. They need to understand: the news is almost entirely controlled by the Left. A One World organization is in control of the American Left. Deep State is real. They hate Christians and they hate Jews. The violence isn't a few random wackos. I've been quietly doing some research and...." She paused and slid the thick copy of *The Times* across the table to Jack. "I've lost a lot of friends over this."

Bette glanced at Tabitha's left hand. No ring. "You were engaged last time we saw you."

"Ryan. He's one of those friends I lost. He called me a nut-job, conspiracy theorist. And that was that."

"What now?" Jack asked.

"I didn't dare put what I know on my computer or send this as an email. I wrote the details out long hand for you to take to the Israeli embassy. It's all there, tucked into the newspaper."

Jack glanced at the newspaper, then at the man filming their conversation. "Can you give it to me in a nutshell?"

She replied, "This is only the beginning. The riots. The arson. It's not mere coincidence. What has been happening around the world. The persecution of Christians and Jews. The burning of Notre Dame in Paris. Now the burning of the ancient Cathedral of Peter and Paul in Nantes, in France. San Gabriel right here before your eyes. Santo Niño Parish. Across the world. They are all arson. No accidents. What we are witnessing now in America; riots, looting, burning. Murder. The killing of cops. It's all related. This is a replay of the French Revolution. Reign of Terror, 1792. In the name of freedom, the French started out beheading statues of saints on the churches, and ended up beheading thousands of people who didn't agree with them. Same with the Bolshevik Revolution 1917. Same years as the flu pandemic. And Germany 1930s; Krystal Nacht. The Nazis used false flags. Set fires. Blamed the Jews for arson, when it was the Nazis themselves who orchestrated the events."

Bette folded the L.A. newspaper and slipped it into her bag. "How can we help you?" Bette asked.

Relief filled Tabitha's eyes. "I'm going to resign from *The Times*. It will be a big deal. Public. I'm going to be Tweeting reasons why I'm leaving. I can't make all the details public, but I will talk about the corruption in the media. That is reason enough. And then I've got to have a safe place to go. Understand? Here in SoCal first, then I'll need to get out of the U.S. fast."

"The Israeli Consulate."

"Yes." She looked down at her hands that were folded as if in prayer. "I'm proud to be an American. But I can't stay here in L.A. Can't stay in America. I know too much. I mean, I need to get back to Israel. Can you arrange that?"

Jack nodded. "I think you should wait and resign after you're safe behind Israeli gates. Don't push 'send' on your resignation letter until you know you're in."

She looked up sharply. "Okay. When?"

"Now. We'll stay with you."

Tabitha grasped her backpack. "I need to stop by home. Can you follow me there? Get my computer. A few clothes. My cat. I can't leave her. I can bring my cat?"

Bette laughed. "She's a Jewish cat. She'll be welcome in Jerusalem."

✿ ✿ ✿

The tall man with the slick hair and the gleaming white smile welcomed Brahim Rahman into a smaller private office in the state house. "Mister Rahman?" he said as his private secretary bowed her way out of the room and closed the door behind her. "You are here at the personal request of Mister….?"

"Please," Rahman cautioned, interrupting. "You must call me Brahim. As for our mutual friend in Hungary—perhaps it is better if we do not refer to his name."

"As you wish. But I have met with him many times and assured him of my gratitude for his support. How can I be of assistance today?"

"Your state has suffered from the virus restrictions," Rahman noted. "Decreased state revenue, loss of jobs, increased benefit payments, increased health care expenses."

"But I thought this was planned; all part of what…."

"Please." Rahman repeated a warning gesture. "You have done well and you will be rewarded for your excellent service. There remains an incomplete part of our—friendship."

"Name it," the governor with the manikin-perfect features asserted.

"The churches," Rahman said. "You have begun to allow businesses to reopen: restaurants, taverns, night clubs. But this must not apply to churches. They must stay empty. It is not important if they carry on with electronic sermons, but the members must become discouraged with the lack of assembly."

"How can I prevent it if thousands of unmasked protestors are allowed to march in the streets?"

Rahman shrugged. "Surely as able and practiced a

diplomat as yourself can determine a means. Protests are out doors; in open air. Churches are closed boxes."

"Yes, yes," the head of one of the world's most prosperous entities said with building excitement. "Limit the number who can attend. Continue to forbid singing; singing spreads the virus. Threaten violating pastors with jail time. Shut off power and water to churches that won't comply. I see it now."

"Of course you do," Rahman agreed. "And your economy—once the envy of the world…."

"Once the fifth largest in the world," the governor corrected. "My state's economy was bigger even than that of the United Kingdom."

"And will be again," Rahman laughed. "As soon as all has been accomplished. In the meantime—surely there are some campaign funds that would benefit from our support? Some political action committees?"

The state official only saved himself from gleefully rubbing his hands together by brushing them down the creases of his perfectly tailored trousers. "You won't be disappointed," he promised.

"Our friend in Hungary is certain you mean that," Rahman confirmed.

✿ ✿ ✿

Tabitha Vanderhorst's voice on Jack's cell phone was choked with tears. On the drive to her apartment she elaborated further on the deception of the media and the way it had sheltered evil.

"There are names. A long list. All the way up through the chain of corporations and governments to the top, and people whose goal is to hide the truth about their own corruption while they bring American democracy and Israel to destruction." She instructed Jack and Bette, "Begin with page forty-two. Personal texts and emails. Documentation of vast international pedophilia rings. They trade kids like baseball cards. There is a list of politicians linked to Epstein. They all hate Trump. They all fear him. After all, on camera, Trump called Epstein's island a cesspool back in 2015. The link to that video is in my report. Trump promised he would drain the swamp and believe me, the swamp creatures are terrified of him, and terrified of the Israeli Prime Minister."

Jack agreed. "The international media has conducted a propaganda campaign to bring down both governments."

"All connected. All of it," the journalist concurred. "This is an international conspiracy. It is profoundly evil. A propaganda machine that rivals Goebbels and the Nazis. Present day, they are as anti-Israel as the Nazis when they were burning Torah scrolls and Bibles in the streets of Berlin before the war. Burn Bibles and churches first, and then they will burn people."

Bette interjected. "How much of this information do they know you have?"

Vanderhorst answered, "We should assume they know

what I have. Otherwise why would they want me dead?" She added, "I have left two copies of these documents in safe places. If I am killed I have left specific instructions as to where they are and who should receive the copies."

Jack stared at the phone for a long moment. It was hard to believe that anyone could be so calm when speaking of the possibility of her own death. "It must not come to that."

She responded, "Have you counted the number of political 'suicides' over the last few years? Somebody needs to inform the public that the child sex trafficking, orgies, and perversion happening on the highest levels has never been just about sex. It has always been about political control. Extortion. Entrapment."

"Blackmail."

"Exactly," she confirmed. "Epstein and the island orgies are part of something much more sinister. I'll say it again. It's global. You get it? The things that happened there and the people who took part in it were all filmed. And now? These BLM riots? Looting? The demonstrations? The global pandemic was meant to shut down churches. Isolate people. All of it is timed to distract and conceal what is really happening here. Anyone in the media who is bought and paid for won't mention that Bill Clinton is on the flight logs of Epstein's pedo-island over twenty-five times. Or that he ditched his security details to go to an orgy. Look at the American government's anti-Israel policies during the administrations of Clinton and Obama. They are owned."

Jack and Bette exchanged grim looks. Bette said quietly. "There is only one place you will be safe."

"I was hoping you would say that." And then she added. "Someone needs to know that I'm not a person who would ever commit suicide. Get it? If ever I turn up dead...."

Jack said, "Let's make sure that never happens."

"One more thing," the journalist added. "Expect major attacks against churches across Europe and America. I am guessing attacks in several cities. There have been orders from the media moguls that certain reporters should be pulled back from cities. Beirut for instance. There's been some sort of tip that something big is about to come down in Lebanon. *The Times* correspondent was ordered out of the city with instructions to stay within an hour's drive of Beirut. That can mean only one thing."

✡ ✡ ✡

Traffic on the 405 Freeway moved at a crawl. Tabitha Vanderhorst's bright red Toyota Corolla was two cars in front of the non-descript, white rental car Jack drove.

"I forgot why I hate L.A. so much." Jack drummed his fingers on the steering wheel. "Traffic. I could walk faster."

"At least her car is red," Bette said. "She probably doesn't have a clue where we are, but I've got my eye on her." A few minutes later Bette fell asleep and Jack was navigating on his own.

The sun had set by the time the red Corolla turned off on the 10 freeway towards Santa Monica. Jack flashed his lights as he came up on her tail. She responded in kind, then turned on her blinker and exited at the Lincoln off ramp.

Bette opened her eyes and sat up abruptly. "What happened?"

"It's the middle of the night in Europe and we're in California. Jet lag."

"Sorry. I'm so tired." Bette spotted the red flash of Tabitha's vehicle. "There she is."

Another five minutes of side streets and they pulled up in front of a condo complex. Tabitha stepped out and stood at the curb. "I'm sorry. Terrible traffic. 405 is a nightmare any time, but we hit the worst. Construction on Century Boulevard. I probably should have gone frontage streets, but you never know if they'll be just as terrible."

Jack's head was pounding from accumulated jet lag. "It's okay. No surprise. I lived here too. Let's go."

Tabitha locked her car and hurried toward her condo. Inserting the keys, she pushed open the door and switched on the lights at the same moment.

She gave a little cry. "Oh no! No! What have they done!"

Jack held Bette back with one hand and peered over Tabitha's shoulder at the wreckage of what had been a tidy little home.

Couches and chairs were overturned. The bottom fabric was shredded. Drawers were emptied onto the floor.

Dishes flung out of the cupboards were shattered in pieces on the tile.

Aware that the burglars might be armed and hiding inside, Jack pulled Tabitha out of the house beside Bette and closed the door.

"We're not going in there."

Tabitha was already calling 9-1-1, and was giving her address to the dispatcher. She hung up. "Cops are on the way. They told me not to go in."

Jack felt the rush of danger. What if this was not a simple break in? "Look. We're leaving now. Go. Get in the car."

Tabitha protested, "I can't! My cat!"

"We've got to get you to the Israeli Consulate," he whispered hoarsely as he pictured the headline: LOS ANGELES TIMES REPORTER KILLED BY ROBBER. As convenient for the enemy as claiming she was a suicide.

Before Jack could object, Tabitha flung the condo door open and called for her cat. "Harpo! Harpo!"

With a pitiful meow, an enormous yellow tabby climbed from the wreckage and leapt into Tabitha's arms.

"Now," Jack insisted. "Go!"

They left the door wide open for the police, and drove away without looking back.

✡ ✡ ✡

In the rear view mirror Jack glimpsed the flashing lights of a patrol car round the corner on the call to Tabitha's shattered condo. He was aware of the headlights of a black SUV with tinted windows pulling away from the curb as they passed.

From the back seat Tabitha held her cat and asked nervously, "Do you think we're being followed?"

Jack did not reply at first. He turned left on a residential street, then made a quick right at the corner. The SUV stayed with them. Another left turn into Pico Boulevard traffic. Jack maneuvered into the far left lane, leaving the SUV in the right lane and two cars back.

"Yes," Jack answered. "We're being followed." He was grateful for their non-descript white rental car; grateful for the bumper-to-bumper traffic of Pico Boulevard. "We'll ditch them at the light."

Tabitha, breathless, looked over her shoulder at the pursuer. "I didn't expect this. Not so quickly. I thought there was time."

The SUV put on its blinker and bullied its way through the tangle of cars toward them. The light changed and Jack accelerated forward, but then a string of red taillights lit up as the cars all ground to a halt at once.

The pursuers were still a few car lengths back, but the black vehicle barred the last exit from the congestion ahead.

"What is it?" Tabitha seemed on the edge of panic.

Bette peered forward. "Demonstrators! Blocking the street!"

BLM signs bounced above a massive crowd in the

intersection. The blare of air horns and beating drums mixed with primal chants,

"KILL THE COPS!"

"DEFUND THE POLICE!"

"BLACK LIVES MATTER! BLACK LIVES MATTER!"

Drivers on the leading edge of the blocked traffic honked and tried to ease their way through. The mob erupted in fury, leaping onto hoods, and smashing vehicle windows with skateboards and baseball bats.

Tabitha screamed as the wave of violence swept closer. Jack saw the car door of the SUV thrown open. Two men, one enormous and another, leaner and a little shorter, jumped out and stood assessing the situation. Both wore windbreakers. Each had a hand thrust inside a jacket.

Armed men, ready to kill.

Rioters ahead and coming closer.

Thugs behind, blocking escape toward the rear.

"Jack?" Bette queried calmly. "What do we do?"

A quick prayer and Jack was suddenly struck with inspiration. "Stay put 'til I see if this works," he ordered.

Emerging from the rental car and standing on the doorframe, Jack shouted and waved toward the advancing rioters: "BLACK LIVES MATTER! Hey! That car! The black SUV! Right back there! Those guys! Undercover cops! They're cops! Look! They're undercover cops!"

Like a swarm of hornets the mob coalesced and flowed in a demonic rage toward the SUV.

"Get back, you stupid morons!" Jack heard one of the hired thugs bellow, just before he was swarmed by half-a-dozen sign-wielding rioters.

The other assassin didn't wait to be assaulted. From inside his windbreaker he produced a pistol and fired into the air.

The mob shrieked and split in different directions.

"Hold on!" Jack shouted, ducking back inside. "Now's our chance!" Throwing the car into reverse and smashing the vehicle behind them, he created enough space to turn. Cranking the wheel hard to the left, he bumped his front wheels onto the sidewalk and inched forward as mad, howling, creatures in black jumped onto the hood of the car and began to pound on the roof and shatter the glass.

"Get down! Bette! Tabitha! Get down!" The window on the back passenger side broke. A black-gloved hand penetrated the compartment, grabbing Tabitha's hair. Bette leveled a karate chop on the attacker's forearm, snapping the bone against the window frame. He howled like a wounded wolf and fell back, taking down four others with him.

More shots erupted into the air behind them. With a noise like the blow from a sledge-hammer, something hit the car's rear.

Foot-by-painfully-slow-foot, Jack continued their advance onto the sidewalk between a Subway sandwich shop and a lamppost.

Policemen in riot gear roared up as Jack guided the

automobile onto the asphalt of a side street. From there they made good their escape.

☆ ☆ ☆

The gates of the Israeli Consulate closed behind the battered vehicle. A wall of consulate sentries closed around them.

Tabitha wept quietly in the back seat as she cradled her dead cat. "I think they were aiming at me," she sobbed, as a tall, muscled IDF officer took the limp animal from her.

Jack locked eyes with the Chief of Security and nodded. What Tabitha said was true.

Bette, clutching the satchel containing Tabitha's dossier on the media's Global connections, embraced her. "I'm so sorry, Tabitha. Come along. Come along, now."

Bette handed Tabitha over to a gentle, doe-eyed consulate nurse, instructing her in Hebrew, "Her name is Tabitha Vanderhorst. She is not wounded. The blood is from her cat, killed in the attack. She's very traumatized, as you can see. Please take good care of her."

The nurse encircled Tabitha with her arm and spoke in broken English as one would address a small child. "Come now, my dear girl. We have a very nice suite for you upstairs. A nice hot bath and clean clothes."

"I didn't bring my clothes. Only Harpo. Oh, look! Blood! They shot Harpo, but it was me they were after. Poor Harpo!"

"Not to worry." The nurse led her toward the elevator. "We have extra things for you to wear. But first a good night's sleep."

"You won't leave me, will you?"

"No. I'll stay with you. Right beside your door."

Tabitha, her eyes red and swollen, looked up at Bette and raised her hand in farewell as the elevator doors slid shut.

Jack and Bette were ushered into an elegant salon and offered chicken sandwiches as Morrie Ryskin, the section head of intelligence, was called. He was an old friend of Bette, and knew Jack well enough to approve of him.

Ryskin pulled up a chair and sat down without formality. "So? You two desperados arrive in America and drive right into the middle of a riot?"

Jack swigged a bottle of lime-flavored Perrier, suddenly realizing how thirsty he was. "We leave Paris to meet with her, and then this. Welcome home to America, eh?"

Morrie cleaned his glasses. "The new normal, I'm afraid."

"We were being followed. Or rather, Tabitha Vanderhorst was being pursued. Her condo was ransacked. They were looking for this." Jack gestured for Bette to produce the document.

Bette removed Tabitha's report from her backpack and placed it on the table.

Jack slid the folder toward Morrie. "We haven't read it. But from what she told us, it's one of those connect the dots puzzles. She's documented the media connection to the Deep State. Global. From what she said—and there was a whole lot she told us—it's all connected: from the rise of anti-Semitism, to the plague, to the riots, to the attempt to impeach Trump. I gather this is the closest America has ever come to a presidential coup."

Morrie flipped through the document. His face grew hard as he stopped to silently read. With a nod, he snapped the cover closed. "She names names. No wonder they want her dead."

"She's pretty shook up," Bette interjected. "The riot was bad enough even without the fact that she was being followed."

Jack added, "She'll need to leave the US."

Morrie agreed. "Of course. We'll get her on a flight to Israel as soon as it can be arranged." His eyes narrowed. "You'll be staying with us awhile?"

"We've got a suite at the Beverly Wilshire," Jack explained. "But we'll need another car, I think. Would you explain the smashed car to Avis for us?"

"Finish your sandwich. I'll have someone drive you over. You need some sleep. Might be a good idea to give you a team of bodyguards at the hotel. You'll never know they're there. So, well done. Go get some sleep. We can talk this over tomorrow."

✿ ✿ ✿

A basket of fruit was on the inlaid marble table of room 252. The king-sized bed at the Beverly Wilshire Hotel was turned back and ready. Plush robes and slippers, embroidered with the hotel logo, were laid out and ready for Jack and Bette.

They showered and fell onto the bed in exhaustion. Both stared blankly at the ornately-coved ceiling.

"How long has it been since I kissed you?" Jack asked hoarsely.

"I don't know."

"Too long."

"Uh-huh."

Jack leaned over and pecked her on the cheek. "I'll do better later." He started to reach up and switch off the lamp.

Bette stopped him. "Wait. Please. Don't turn out the light."

"What is it?"

"Jack, would you mind if we slept with the light on? One light. Maybe just the bathroom light?"

"Sure, babe. No problem. Are you okay?"

"No. I'm really not okay, I guess."

"We've got two consulate body guards looking after us." Jack tried to console her. "No human is getting through that door."

"It's not that. I know nothing—human—could." She emphasized the word "human," and then fell silent.

"What is it, Bette? What are you trying to say?"

"Jack? I know this is going to sound crazy."

"Try me."

"Well, I'm afraid you'll think I am insane."

"After what we've been through, nothing will shock me or make me think anything. I mean, you broke that guy's arm when he reached in. What a wonder woman you are."

"Listen." She hesitated. "I saw things in the mob."

"Okay. Want to talk about it?"

"I mean I saw creatures. Horrible, hideous creatures. Not human. They inhabited the rioters. Their faces were evil, Jack. And there were more of them than there were actual humans. Some leapt from the heads of the rioters. Others sat on their backs and as the people shouted, the mouths of the creatures moved, mouthing exactly the same words. The arm that grabbed at us? Its hand was a claw."

A cold chill swept over Jack. He had witnessed demons himself. This was exactly what Bette was describing. "Can you tell me what they looked like?"

"One had an ugly, evil-looking neck and a bird's head. Another had a face like a pig."

"I get it, I get it," Jack reassured her. "I don't think you're crazy. I've seen them too. What I saw happened two hundred years ago—but the same monsters." Jack paused to hug Bette before continuing. "Bette, we are covered by the blood of our Savior, Jesus Christ. Demons can't harm us. Say it. In the Name of Jesus. No evil can come near me."

Bette repeated, "In the Name of Jesus. No evil can come near me. I believe that, Jack. I know that it's true. I saw a great light come between us and the dark creatures. Protection. Like a wall of light."

"Angels."

"Yes. Yes. That must have been what I saw. But the other creatures were so horrible. I suddenly realized that this is a war, not simply for the survival of America and Israel! This is a spiritual war between Good and Evil. A war for the souls of men. There is Light fighting against profound Darkness—and spiritual beings who are warring all around us."

Jack responded quietly, "I read this again just the other day. In Ephesians: 'We wrestle not against flesh and blood but against principalities and powers,' and—you know—'the spiritual forces of evil.'"

"Yes. That is what I saw. I think something has escaped from hell. It is taking over the bodies of humans, like a bad science-fiction movie. Only Jack, it's true!" She covered her face with both hands and sighed. "And I'm so tired!"

Jack gathered her in his arms and pulled her close. He kissed her forehead. "It's almost 1:00am. Just sleep now, babe. I've got you. Just rest a while. Think of the angels who came to fight for us. God is watching over us."

She lay in the crook of his arm; her head on his chest. He stroked her hair until her body relaxed. Only then did he let himself drift off to sleep.

✡ ✡ ✡

An IDF driver picked up Jack and Bette at the Beverly Wilshire Hotel and drove them back to the Israeli Consulate, where they were promised their new rental car.

Morrie Ryskin had a continental breakfast and coffee for them in his office.

Jack remarked, "The Pico riot didn't even make the news."

"Nothing really happened—according to the media. It was a 'peaceful protest.'"

Bette cradled her mug. "Our car was smashed. Shots fired. That's nothing?"

Morrie shrugged, "There were nineteen black-on-black murders in Chicago last weekend. That barely makes the news. Nobody died on Pico."

"Not for want of trying," Jack drily replied.

Morrie finished his apricot Danish. "If they had killed Tabitha Vanderhorst and then escaped she would have been one more 'accidental' death by shooting in a whole string of so-called accidents. There are prominent conservatives who are at severe risk right now. *The Times* would have put her obit on the back page and moved on."

Bette asked, "Is she okay?"

Morrie replied. "She will be. On her way back to Israel at 4:00 this morning."

"Her dossier must be important." Jack frowned.

"International. Too many prominent players in the American Left connected to bad actors for her to be able to live. Really bad. China. Iran. This has been a serious attempted coup against the president and an attempt to drive Israel into the sea at the same time. If you hadn't met with her when you did she would be just another 'suicide' in a long list of suicides. And it isn't over yet."

Bette pressed her lips together. "Okay. So there's more. You didn't just ask us here for breakfast, Morrie. There's more you want from us. Spill it."

Morrie nodded and directed his comment to Jack. "I keep forgetting you've been to the rodeo."

Jack gave a strained laugh. "This is supposed to be our honeymoon, not a rodeo."

"Business and pleasure. The perfect cover." Morrie spread his hands and shrugged in a gesture of innocence. "Well, okay then. Here it is: We'd like you to attend a meeting at the Hoover Institute at Stanford. You know several of the members from your time with the Middle Eastern think tank."

"We were on opposite sides of the table back then," Jack replied. "But sure. Agreed. To what end?"

"They are preparing a report for the president about America and Israel. Next steps. You're now on the right side of the table. The riots here are not just staged to divide and destroy America, but Israel as well. You'll be an asset—and Bette as well. You both have a lot to contribute, personally."

"When?"

"Three days. Drive up the coast. Take your time. The governor is trying to shut down California again. Most counties—even the central coast—San Luis Obispo County, several small beach towns. The sheriff there is ignoring the governor's orders; he refuses to arrest people for walking on the beaches. There've been no riots. Quiet and out-of-the-way mission town. Wine country. Most of their vineyard technology comes from Israel. Great connection. It's half way between here and Stanford. Then you can drive up Highway 1 through Big Sur and Monterey. Beautiful. And it's on us. An offer you can't refuse?"

Bette finished her coffee and glanced at Jack to read his agreement. "Jack?"

Jack was silent a long moment. "We've already been through the worst. What can go wrong?"

10

IF MY PEOPLE....

The Israeli Consulate provided Jack and Bette with a white, all-wheel-drive Pathfinder. Jack was also given a new cell phone and three emergency phone numbers in case help was needed. He was told a fob on the key chain would detect bugs or tracking devices on the car or in any hotel rooms.

They were left on their own to find random hotels in which to stay along the coastal route north. There was only one thing left for Jack to do to assure they could not be traced or pursued by anyone. He jotted down the consulate emergency numbers and shoved the paper into his pocket.

"You know the Prime Minister of Israel doesn't carry a cell phone?" Jack pulled into the turnout on the mountainous two-lane road overlooking Santa Barbara.

"Smart man." Bette smiled. "Beautiful view. You would think there was no one in the whole world but us. But, at the risk of sounding paranoid, you know the consulate can listen in on the cell phone whenever they want. Inhibiting, to say the least."

"True," Jack agreed. The two climbed out of the vehicle and stood hand-in-hand in silence for a moment as the sun sank low above the Channel Islands, and the sea turned silver. "Shall we?"

Jack handed Bette the consulate cell phone that she jammed beneath the treads of the back wheel. Jack started the car and rolled forward, pinning the cell phone as if it was a rattlesnake in the road.

There was something satisfying about the sound of crunching glass and metal.

"Nice," Bette stooped to examine the destruction.

They watched the sun set over the argent Pacific with a sense of contentment. Retrieving the crushed remnants of the phone, Jack heaved it high and away off the rocky precipice.

"Now we are truly alone." Bette kissed him.

Driving back down the crooked mountain road, they cruised along the waterfront and checked into Santa Barbara's Harbor Inn. They strolled onto Stern's Wharf and found a table beneath the stars at Woody's Longboard café.

Waves crashed against the pilings of the pier. Bette leaned across the table and whispered, "Jack I don't remember ever feeling quite so free. At least not for a very long time. It's delicious. Better than food."

The last rays of light shone on her smooth olive skin. Full lips curved in a gentle smile. "Delicious. That's you. Delirious. That's me."

He wanted nothing but her. Throw the world away with the cell phone. Find some little hidden house in the hills; plant a vineyard, make wine, and babies. Nothing else in life seemed to matter.

"Are you hungry?" he asked.

"We can order to go. Eat in the room. Stay up all night. Make love. Sleep. Wake. Make love. Sleep. Watch *Sleepless in Seattle*."

The amused waitress, unnoticed, stood over them, waiting; taking it in. "You guys sure you want dinner?"

Bette laughed. "Well, maybe not here. Better take it to our room. Two Big Bopper Burgers and fries to go. Two chocolate shakes. And cherry cheesecake for later?" She winked at Jack. "Good?"

"Good."

✿ ✿ ✿

The Harbor Inn's blackout curtains were drawn. Bette was sleeping away her exhaustion when Jack got up and dressed. He scrawled Bette a note, then left her crashed in the hotel room.

"Back soon. Seeing to a few small details. Just you and

me, kid. Making sure we'll have more uninterrupted nights like last night."

An envelope stuffed with hundred dollar bills, which he had stashed in the lining of his suitcase, was used to purchase ten $500 Visa gift cards from different grocery stores around Santa Barbara.

His final stop was a Target department store where he purchased a pre-paid, disposable flip phone with primitive talk/text capability only. The technology was at least ten years old. As simple as you could get. No Wi-Fi. No blue tooth. The clerk did not ask for Jack's identification. The disposable phone was untraceable.

Jack sat in the car outside the lobby and entered the three emergency numbers into the phone.

"Just in case," he told himself.

But in case of what?

Bette was still sleeping when he returned. He retrieved his note and threw it away. She would never even know he had been gone.

He fixed himself a cup of coffee.

As the aroma filled the room, she stirred, raised her head and asked, "Why are you dressed? What are you doing making coffee in the middle of the night?"

"Blackout curtains. It's day."

"What time?" she whispered.

"Almost noon, Mrs. Garrison."

She raised up on her elbows. "Not possible. Jack? Noon? Really? Somewhere it's midnight. Midnight in

Paris. Or Israel. But I don't want to dream about any place but here. And about you."

"Dream as long as you like. I'll be here when you wake up. Go back to sleep."

"What are you going to do?"

"No internet, remember? I'm going to run down to the lobby and pick up a newspaper."

She waved her hand in a languid goodbye, then turned over and burrowed her head into the pillow.

Jack resisted the urge to laugh. Bette was going to be fun to be married to.

He hurried to catch the elevator. As the doors slid open, a small crowd of guests stood transfixed in the lobby. They stared up at a screen as clips of a cataclysmic explosion roared on the screen.

"Beirut!" someone exclaimed.

"Looks like a nuclear bomb!"

"How could anyone survive that?"

"Merciful God!"

"Reminds me of 9-11."

Jack did not wait for the elevator, but bounded up the stairs and into the room. He clicked on the news. The destruction of Beirut was on every channel.

Bette sat up and watched in silent horror. Every video was a different angle captured on the cell phones from the window of ordinary people.

Neither Jack nor Bette spoke for a long time. At last she said quietly, "Tabitha Vanderhorst mentioned Beirut.

Beirut! Something about the correspondent. She warned us. Jack? She was right!"

"If it can happen there, where else? And when?"

--- ☆ ☆ ☆ ---

It was a very somber road trip for some time after the Beirut news. Even so, after getting a very late start from Santa Barbara, and following a couple hours driving north on Highway 101, Jack was hungry. "You up for some lunch?" he asked.

"Sure. Got any ideas?"

"I asked Morrie Ryskind for suggestions. He said make this a leisurely trip, so how about a bite in Pismo Beach? Place called Mo's?"

"Fine by me," Bette agreed, offering Jack a radiant smile.

"Don't do that!" Jack warned.

"What?"

"Don't smile at me like that while I'm driving. Too much distraction! You want me to run us off the road?"

Frowning severely and lowering her chin, Bette returned, "No, captain. Aye, aye, captain. No more smiles—scowls only."

"Maybe I didn't mean it," Jack returned. "Could be a time to say, 'Jesus, take the wheel?'"

Soon afterward, when both were smiling at the bright sunlight illuminating hillsides covered in lush, green grapevines, they arrived in Pismo Beach, and exited the freeway toward the pier. "Pismo?" Bette inquired.

"Native American word. Also some kind of clam. Lev said it means 'tar' that the early people used to make their canoes sea-worthy. But you know Lev. He might have been pulling my leg."

"He might be—what again?"

"Pulling my leg—English idiom. Means—umm—'teasing me.' In British English, 'Having me on.'"

"I see," Bette said nodding. "*Atah ovayd alie,*" she said in Hebrew. "You're—umm—pulling a job on me?"

"That's it. You've got it."

Bette was smiling again. "Jack. Now I'm pulling a job on *you*. My English is good enough to know, 'pulling your leg.'"

"I'm gonna spank you, child."

"Nope. We're here."

After a meal of shredded barbecued beef, with all the trimmings, Bette and Jack drove along Highway 1, which paralleled the ocean. Horns blared behind them. "Jack! Is it another riot? Should we get out of here?"

Checking out the view in the rearview mirror, Jack replied: "I don't think it's the same thing at all. Look."

Just a block before a side road led down to the sand, a monster truck, horn blaring, roared up behind them. Waving grandly from the bed of the pickup was an oversize American flag.

The giant vehicle was merely the leader of a long

line of similar mammoth off-road-vehicles. Pulling over, Jack let the parade go by. Every one of the ORVs was similarly equipped with flags, or red, white and blue bunting, or sported coiled snake banners proclaiming, "Don't Tread On Me!"

"Nope, not the same at all," Jack said. "Let's go watch."

The audio speakers of the heroically-sized leading vehicle blared, "I'm Proud to be an American," as it led the procession onto the beach. One after another, flag-waving, proud Americans paraded up and down miles of packed sand by the waters' edge.

"There must be two hundred of them," Bette said, marveling.

"And there's something else going on down at the water's edge," Jack noted. Black and white, brown, and mixed race, a crowd of a couple thousand barefoot, shorts-and-tee shirt wearing on-lookers, anti-viral masks pulled down around their necks, formed a semi-circular audience for a black man standing in the bed of a parked truck. "Let's go listen."

"Brothers and sisters!" the man loudly proclaimed. "My name is Pastor Sharp. Now maybe you're here today 'cause you love your country! And that's good! I do too! Land of the Free and Home of the Brave! Can I get an Amen?"

Over the rumble of trucks could be heard shouts of "Amen!"

Nodding his head in approval the preacher continued,

"That's good! That's real good! But today my question for you is: do you love my Jesus?"

The beach resounded with "Amen!" and "Praise the Lord!" and "I do!"

"Jack," Bette said. "I love Jesus. I saw Him."

"I know, babe. He answered my prayer when He saved your life."

"Sing with me," the Pastor Sharp urged. "Everybody say: Way Maker."

The crowd sang in near unison, "Way Maker! Miracle Worker! Promise Keeper! Light in the Darkness, My God! That is Who You Are!"

"Again!"

"Way Maker! Miracle Worker!"

Bette and Jack added their voices to the chorus of praise. "Promise Keeper! Light in the Darkness, My God! That is Who You Are!"

"Raise your hands and sing it out!"

The chorus repeated and repeated without let up for a full five minutes.

"Real Good! Real Good! Now listen to me for just a bit longer!" Sharp requested. "If I call this a 'threshing floor moment,' do you even know what I'm talking about? Jesus said, the time is coming when the threshers will separate the wheat from the chaff—the true believers from the social Christians, from the 'go-along-to-get-along' crowd. A threshing floor moment has come upon the world, brothers and sisters. It's here now—today.

"Taking the long view, I mean, the eternal view, it doesn't matter if you're black or white. It doesn't matter if you're rich or poor. It doesn't matter if you've been to college or not. What matters is: do you know Jesus? Is He Your Lord and Savior? Like Brother Paul said in his letter to the Romans: 'If you confess with your mouth the Lord Jesus and believe in your heart that God has raised Him from the dead, you will be saved.'

"Brother and sisters, will you follow Him, wherever He leads? Today is the acceptable day of salvation, the Bible says. What are you waiting for?"

Pastor Sharp extended his arms in a wide gesture of welcome that encompassed both the crowd and the Pacific Ocean. "Like the man in the chariot said to Philip the Evangelist: 'Here's water. What doth hinder me to be baptized?' Who's ready?"

"Jack," Bette said. "I want to do this. Me. I want to do this today. Will you go with me?"

"Of course I will, Bette."

And just like that they joined a line of over a hundred people waiting a turn to go down into the water and come up laughing and singing and praising God.

"Thank you," Bette said to Pastor Sharp after she was baptized.

His face split into the widest possible grin. Beaming at her he said, "You are so welcome! Thank *you*! Thanks for trusting God—and me—with this big, important step."

IF MY PEOPLE....

✿ ✿ ✿

Comet Neowise hung in the sky to the northwest of Morro
Bay, California. From a hilltop a few miles south of and
high above the seaside community there was plenty of dark
sky for the interplanetary visitor to be visible by eye alone.
Jack and Bette breathed the salt air off the ocean as it min-
gled with the sharp bite of creosote brush. Both sighed
with relief at being free, at least for the moment, from the
madness gripping the world.

"Six thousand years, they say," Jack remarked, gesturing
at the comet's bright head and fainter, curved tail. "To see
it again we'd have to still be around in six millennia or so.
Shall we book it now?"

"Jack," Bette remarked. "Where will you be in six thousand years? Where will I be? I'm pretty sure we will have
even more exciting things to see and do by then."

"Not so fast there," Jack retorted cheerfully. "What
could be more exciting than this: here I am with the most
gorgeous gal in the galaxy, that I'm just about to kiss...."

Moments passed before either spoke again, then
Bette turned away from Jack and back toward the comet.
Wrapping Jack's arms around herself she snuggled against
him. "Jack," she said, "Do you think comets mean anything? Spiritual, I mean?"

"Are we getting serious?"

"Not if you'd rather not," Bette returned agreeably.

Resting his chin on the top of her head, he inhaled her fragrance—jasmine—and replied, "In fairness, I was wondering the same thing. Blood moons, two annular eclipses six months apart—now this. You know, I have learned to say…."

"Everything means something," Bette concluded for him.

"All right, smarty. So what do you think?"

"No, not me. What did Yeshua say?"

Jack thought for a moment. "I asked Lev about it. He quoted Jesus as recorded in the Gospel of Luke: 'And there will be signs in the sun, in the moon, and in the stars; and on earth distress of nations, with perplexity, the sea and the waves roaring; men's hearts failing them for fear and the expectation of those things which are coming on the earth, for the powers of the heavens will be shaken.'"

When spoken beneath the pale glow of the comet, and while standing barely three hours away from rioting and assassination attempts—nothing seemed to still be lacking to fulfill Jesus' words.

Bette shivered.

"Are you cold, babe? I'm sorry. Should we go?"

"No, no, Jack. I was just wondering—maybe we won't have to wait for another comet to find out what's coming next. Maybe we'll know sooner than that."

✿ ✿ ✿

After raising a hallelujah on a California beach, getting baptized in the Pacific Ocean, witnessing a once in forever celestial visitor—somehow, Jack was not surprised that this was a night for visions as well.

Cold winds swirled over a mountain peak. The white dome of an observatory slowly opened, revealing the lens of an enormous telescope. Clouds spread out beneath them like the sea, concealing the landscape thousands of feet below.

"Where are we?" Jack asked Eliyahu.

"The top of the world," the prophet answered cryptically. "As close as man can get to the heavens on his own with his feet still upon the earth."

The night sky shimmered with more stars than Jack had ever seen before. The sight was beautiful and peaceful, yet somehow ominous.

"Why have you brought me here?"

"This is the night when mankind will look up and see destruction hurtling through space on its way to a direct impact with earth."

"An asteroid?"

"Then the second angel blew his trumpet" Eliyahu quoted, "and something like a great mountain burning with fire was thrown into the sea, and a third of the sea became blood."

"I have heard of the near-Earth asteroids. They pass our planet often. Mostly they are unseen, and mankind is unaware how close they come to striking the earth."

"Asteroids have hit before. But none like this. The size of this one is enormous. It is named Apophis the Destroyer, the Lord of Chaos. Its trajectory is known. The date it will hit the earth is known. And all the nations will suddenly discover how small and helpless they are."

"When?" Jack asked. The certainty of Eliyahu's prediction caused a chill of fear to course through him.

"Soon." Eliyahu stretched forth his hand and pointed upward, directing Jack's gaze skyward toward the suddenly visible form of a luminous ball with a menacing orange glow. "There it is. The Destroyer. And yet the world sleeps."

"How soon?" Jack thought about Bette and her brother, and about all Jack's hopes for a family of his own. How long would life on earth carry on before the trajectory of the asteroid caused it to slam into and snuff out much of civilization?

Eliyahu sighed. "The people of all nations will come together. They will try to fight against it—try to deflect it from its path—but it is already too late. Too late. You see? It is coming. It will come. No mere weapon of man will cause so much death and destruction. It is this uncontrollable mountain from space that will pummel humanity. The Destroyer will come." Eliyahu fixed his eyes on the thing.

Suddenly they stood atop a hillside overlooking the vast Pacific Ocean. In the moonlight, Jack recognized the location on the Central Coast of California. Down a narrow, two-lane road stood the containment domes of a nuclear power plant.

For the first time, Jack noticed how similar the nuclear domes were to those of astronomical observatories.

"This place is called Diablo," Eliyahu explained. "Spanish for Devil. And so it is well named. See there: the Diablo power plant stands on the very edge of the sea. When Apophis strikes, part of the sea will evaporate, causing violent storms like none the world has ever known. The coastlines will be destroyed when the waters recede, exposing the ocean floor, because then tsunamis will rush in. Islands will vanish. There is no shoreline around the world that will not be ravaged. In this place, the futile steel and concrete vessels of Diablo will be struck, shattered, and consumed by a wall of water hundreds of feet tall. The radioactive contents of these domes and other nuclear plants around the world will spill out and will poison one third of the sea.

Jack pleaded, "Is there no stopping this? No turning the thing away?"

Eliyahu replied, "It is written. And it will be done."

"How much time do we have?"

"Time is up."

✧ ✧ ✧

Jack followed Eliyahu along a row of three-story, brick townhouses. Shod draft horses pulled freight-laden wagons. The clatter of hooves and iron wheels on cobblestones was almost deafening. Men dressed in knee britches, long coats, and three corner hats wove through the crowded the lanes. Snatches of conversation were mostly British in accent, and yet the words used were a mixture of King James English and a dozen other nationalities.

Jack noted that the buildings looked much like the 18th century brick houses that still existed in London, but the bricks were clean and untarnished by centuries of weather and coal soot. "Where are we?" Jack asked, as they approached a merchant's shop with a sign above the door in the shape of a steaming cup.

"New York City," Eliyahu replied, slipping into the shop behind a pair of wigged, young businessmen. "1719."

The delicious aroma of hot cocoa filled the air. The room was crowded with customers sitting close together at round tables. Discussing commerce and shipping, they sipped thick, dark, steaming cocoa from demitasse cups.

Wooden bins, filled with uncut bricks of chocolate in a variety of colors from light to dark, lined the wall behind a counter. A quartette of aproned clerks measured out spices and weighed chunks of chocolate, collecting payment in silver coins.

Anticipating Jack's question, Eliyahu nodded toward a man negotiating a large export shipment of chocolate to England. "The owner of this business is a Sephardic Jew named Aaron. He is the ancestor of your friend Lev. He became very rich making chocolate and shipping it to Europe. It was he who first blended sugar with bitter cocoa. He helped build the first synagogue in America." Eliyahu indicated a tall, broad-shouldered man of middle age. Angular features, olive skin, dark eyes and hair betrayed his Sephardic ancestry.

"Why bring me here?"

"From the beginning of this nation the offspring of Abraham were a part of the foundation of America."

"But how?"

"The question is, rather: Why?"

"Alright, then. Why?"

"Aaron came here from England. Before that his grandfather escaped from the Inquisition in Spain and Portugal. America is the one place where they were not persecuted for their religion."

"Like the man I saw with Columbus."

Eliyahu agreed. "They gathered here to live in peace, and to pray daily for the reestablishment of the nation of Israel. They believed, you see, that what the prophets have written is true. God will gather His people from the farthest corners of the earth, and all will return from exile to restored Israel. As you have seen, America to them was the gate through which the Jews would return to Eretz Israel. They rightly believed that when the ingathering from America to Israel happened, that same generation would see Messiah come."

"But it did not happen in his lifetime."

"No, but his grandson helped to finance the American Revolution in 1776. The First Amendment of the Constitution enabled Jews to freely worship and retain their Jewish identity without fear. From their help given to George Washington in Valley Forge, until today with the president who brought the American Embassy to Jerusalem, the Children of the Stock of Abraham have been integral in establishing the nation of America so that America might be integral in reestablishing the nation of Israel in these last days. This is the Cyrus Mandate. This mandate is to bless Israel.

"In return there is a heavenly mantle spread over only a handful of American presidents. Because America blesses Israel, God blesses America."

"Through a fortune made in selling chocolate," Jack marveled.

"God does have a sense of humor."

Jack's smiled as he began to comprehend the spiritual link of American to Israel. "The blessing of freedom of worship for all."

"The American Constitution has been a heaven-born protection for all who sought refuge in this land. But more than anyone, the persecuted Stock of Abraham have found shelter here." Eliyahu paused. "From Washington to Trump. There is a reason Satan desires to destroy their legacy. It is important that you see and understand from the beginning."

"Time is short."

Eliyahu spread his hands. "Signs in the heavens, Jack. Time is up."

IF MY PEOPLE....

The eerie glow of a bonfire illuminated the city. Jack smelled the acrid aroma of smoke. *Unter den Linden*, a street in the center of Berlin, was draped with Nazi flags. From a broad city square, the roar of a packed mob resounded, amplified against the classical stone buildings.

"You know where we are?" Eliyahu asked as they approached the outer fringe of the jostling crowd of college-aged rioters.

"*Bebelplatz*," Jack answered without hesitation. He knew the place from his travels as a college student. "I remember. After the war it was renamed after the founder of the Social Democratic Party of Germany. I visited in college. I saw the plaque commemorating the Nazi book burning. The place had a feel of evil hovering over it. The name 'Bebel,' reminded me of Beelzebub and also of the Tower of Babel. Tangible Evil. Now I understand."

Eliyahu nodded. "It was once called *Platz am Opernhaus*. In the beginning of Germany's descent into Hitler's grip, the National Socialists burned twenty thousand books here. On the plaque it is written, 'That was only a prelude; where they burn books, they will in the end also burn people.' And yes, later they burned Jews. They burned Christians. They burned anyone who disagreed with them. But do you see the books they are burning?"

Shadows from the flames danced like celebrating

205

demons on the facades and Nazi banners draped on the State Opera and St. Hedwigs's Catholic Cathedral.

Eliyahu reached up and plucked a charred page fragment floating above them. He held it for Jack to examine.

The fragment was printed in old German script. "From a Bible."

Eliyahu read the passage, "Isaiah 2:2. 'And it shall come to pass in the last days, that the mountain of the Lord's house shall be established in the top of the mountains, and shall be exalted above the hills; and all nations shall flow unto it.' This promise from God is immutable. This is why Lucifer hates and fears the Bible above all else."

"And yet people mock God's word," Jack responded.

"We know the end of the story." Eliyahu pointed toward the great cathedral. The double doors were thrown wide. Brown-shirted youths emerged, jeering, their arms loaded with Bibles and prayer books. The crowd cheered, "Heil Hitler," and made a path for the looters as they carried the Bibles to the blazing fire and dumped them onto the roaring flames.

Eliyahu continued, "This was May, 1933. The beginning. From there government-supported rioters in the universities encouraged the desecration. It multiplied and spread from The National Socialist German Students' League, until, at last, the whole world was on fire." Eliyahu took Jack's hand. "Come now."

The thick plume of smoke from the burning volumes rose up and engulfed Jack and Eliyahu, lifting them up like leaves on a roaring wind. Time past was suddenly transposed onto the familiar accents of cursing American rioters. "Black Lives Matter! Black Lives Matter!" Smoke and fires raged all around Jack and Eliyahu. Windows were smashed. The broken statue of George Washington lay face down in a park. A white, male, college-aged rioter urinated on the statue.

In the center of a town square, heaps of Bibles were fed into the leaping flames of a bonfire. The violent mob of black-clad students ran rampant through the streets, smashing shop windows, spray painting slogans on buildings, and setting cars on fire. Profanity was mixed with demonic shrieks for justice and calls for the death of police.

"This is America tonight. ANTIFA. They claimed to be anti-fascists and yet, they are the fascists. Behold! Indeed they are controlled by the same demons as Hitler's fascists two generations ago." With a wave of his hand, Eliyahu swept back a spiritual veil. Jack gasped as thousands of demons swooped above the rioters. The evil spirits perched on the shoulders of young men and women and shrieked the very words that were repeated by the humans they controlled.

"What will happen next?" Jack cried.

"Unless they are stopped by the courage and prayers of the saints, and the repentance of the nation, this is only the beginning." Eliyahu reached up to pluck another charred Bible page from the air. He handed it to Jack. "Read it," he instructed.

Jack took the page and held it up to the light. "Second Timothy 3. 'This know also, that in the last days perilous times shall come. For men shall be lovers of their own selves, covetous, boasters, proud, blasphemers, disobedient to parents, unthankful, unholy, without natural affection, trucebreakers, false accusers, incontinent, fierce, despisers of those that are good....'" Jack raised his eyes and folded the fragment, slipping it into his pocket.

Eliyahu swept his hand across the violent chaos unfolding before them. "And all those evil things have come upon the world as it was predicted. Fear not. The hour is near when every knee shall bow, and every tongue shall confess that Jesus Christ is Lord."

Jack sensed that their time together was coming to an end.

"I believe."

Eliyahu smiled. "It is well that you know these things, my son."

"Can America be saved?"

"It is written: 'If my people, who are called by My name, will repent and humble themselves before the Lord, then their land will be healed.' But hear me again: Time is up."

A white mist encircled the two men, separating Jack from Eliyahu. The prophet stepped back, raised his hand in farewell and vanished. Jack gazed after him for a moment and then fell into a deep, untroubled, sleep.

11

New Faces, Old Demons

After breakfast, Jack scanned the front page of the local
newspaper. "We need to get on the road. There's going to
be a BLM protest march today. Look." He showed Bette
the calendar in the bottom corner of the front page.

"They've scheduled them every day this week," she
replied with surprise. "And yet the state governor has
ordered all the churches closed. How can this be?"

"Likely it will shut down the town. Block the highway."

"Been there, done that. No, thank you. Give me five
minutes." Bette threw her clothes into the suitcase while
Jack notified the front desk they were checking out.

"And since we took an extra day here," Jack said, "I
suppose we better go up the quicker route. 101. Then
we can take our time and come back along the Big Sur

coast. Highway 1. We don't want to have to rush that. Sound good?"

They passed police cars parked at every on and off ramp in the quaint Central Coast community. Looking for news on the car radio about the explosion in Beirut, Jack paused for a few minutes on a local talk show. They listened as angry locals weighed in on the hijacking of their community.

"And now the governor says we can't sing in churches?"

"The governor shuts down our churches, but gives these punks the right to riot in our streets?"

"They're issuing citations to people who go to church! Turning off the churches' water and electricity!"

"Open our schools! These are nothing but a bunch of bored high school kids with nothing else to do."

"Destroying our businesses and our lives!"

"We can all go shop at Walmart, but they've closed down our churches."

Bette switched off the radio. "Enough, Jack. It's all the same. Horrible. Over and over. What's happening here is just the local microcosm of what's happening across the world. People are suffering."

"There's an author we all studied as kids. George Orwell. He wrote about this moment. I mean he must have been prophetic. He warned that obedience to the government is not enough. I knew the quote by heart once." He paused and searched his memory then quoted it verbatim. "'Unless he is suffering, how can you be sure he is obeying your will and not his own? Power is inflicting pain and humiliation. Power is tearing human minds to pieces and putting them together again in new shapes of your own choosing.'"

Bette stared at him. "He was right. It's exactly what is happening."

"The book was called *1984*. His date was early, but Orwell saw this coming."

"What is to be done?" Bette gazed out the window as they passed seemingly endless, lush green vineyards.

"That's what we'll be discussing at Stanford. How to wake up America. Mark Twain said that it's easier to fool people than to convince them they have been fooled. That's what we are dealing with. Maybe there are answers."

Jack was relieved when the town was in the rear view mirror. They had escaped the rioters who threatened to block the highway and bring down a sleepy little town with violence.

Miles slid away with thousands of acres of vines rolling over the hills into the distance.

"Look." Bette pointed to a road sign. "This road has a name. El Camino Royale."

"The King's Highway," Jack translated.

"Beautiful. This reminds me so much of home. Israel's vineyards." Bette thumbed through her Bible to Isaiah 35 and began to read: "The desert will rejoice, and flowers will bloom in the wilderness. The desert will sing and shout for joy. Everyone will see the Lord's splendor, see His greatness and power. Give strength to the hands that are tired and to knees that tremble with weakness. Tell everyone who is discouraged, 'Be strong and don't be afraid! God is coming to your rescue, coming to punish your enemies.' The blind will be able to see, and the deaf will hear. The lame will leap and dance, and those who cannot speak will shout for joy. Streams of water will flow through the desert and the burning sand will become a lake and dry land will be filled with springs. Where jackals used to live, marsh grass and reeds will grow. There will be a highway there, called, 'The Road of Holiness.'"

She kept her Bible open on her lap as they drove. Jack sensed that she was making connections between these vineyards and Israel. He knew that the same drip irrigation systems developed for Israel's vineyards were now used in the vast California grape industry. Israelis had made their deserts bloom. Then, in the early 1970s, seven young Californian farmers had flown to Israel to learn their secret. The Californians had brought home the Israeli irrigation technology and California wine country was the result. The bond between the land of Israel and the present prosperity of American vineyards was undeniable. Present day California without Israel's technology would have remained a dry, agricultural backwater. Now, because of the fulfillment of the ancient prophecy in Isaiah, California's barren hills were blooming.

Bette inhaled deeply. She said quietly, "No wonder the devil fights so hard to take over this place."

"America is a kind of suburb of Israel," Jack agreed.

Bette sighed and changed the subject, "Alright. But I need a change of clothes, remember? T-shirts and sandals?" She reminded Jack as they drove up the 101 Freeway towards Stanford.

✡ ✡ ✡

Jack and Bette intended to break their journey northward on the south side of Monterey Bay, about a half hour off the 101. After a hundred miles driving, a stroll was required before continuing.

"Let me take you to Cannery Row," Jack proposed.

"Cannery Row, as in Steinbeck?" Bette asked.

"The very same," Jack confirmed.

Despite his good intentions, Jack's memory of where to exit the interchange to reach Steinbeck country played him false. Instead of emerging beside Fishermen's Wharf, Jack got entangled in the campus of Junipero Serra College.

JSC was a small, Catholic, liberal arts school in Monterey, California. It had about four hundred undergraduate students, and an additional quarter of that number pursuing master's degrees. Located not far from the spot where the city of Monterey was founded in 1770, the college was empty of students because it was the summer term. Besides, in the wake of the corona virus, almost all classes were being held on-line anyway.

Jack pulled the rental car over in front of the administration building, where its larger than life-size statue of the Franciscan priest stood in a rose garden beside the entry steps. "Larger-than-life-sized," Jake voiced his thoughts. "Pretty easy where Father Serra is concerned."

Bette looked dubious; expecting a joke. "Why?" she demanded suspiciously.

"Because the real guy was only a little over five feet tall. No, really. I looked it up."

"And he is the founder of the California missions?" Bette inquired.

"Nine of them," Jack confirmed. "From Spain, originally. Walked across Mexico, and then up California. Was already fifty-six when he started his mission-building."

"Seriously?" Bette said with admiration. "I thought he'd have to be a young man."

Jack shrugged. "Gave it his all," he said. "Died in 1784 at age seventy after hiking twenty-four thousand miles—about the distance around the earth," Jack mused. "Hadn't thought of that until now. Anyway, according to the Catholic Church, now he's Saint Serra."

"So Christianity was out here in California...."

"Before the United States really got organized as a country," Jack concluded. Glancing in the car's rearview mirror he said, "Oh-oh."

"What? Trouble?"

"Just sit tight. Looks like a protest. Guess leaving San Luis Obispo early wasn't a good enough plan."

From both ends of the block, groups of black-masked

and black-shirted youths converged on the admin struc-
ture. Waving signs reading Black Lives Matter, and
No More White Supremacy, they gathered around the
Serra statue.

Their leader, a heavy-set, white girl, whose purple hair
protruded all around the margins of her black bandana,
held up her hands for silence. "Here is the list of our
demands," she shouted through a portable loudspeaker to
responsive cheers. "We demand the right to protest and be
respected. We demand defunding the police and investing
for people of color. We demand immediate relief for people of color. We demand community control. We demand
an end to the war on people of color, and an end to sys-
temic racism."

Was there a moment when the pointed, whiskery snout
of a rat-like creature appeared to be superimposed on the
girl's mask? Turning toward Bette, by her wide-eyed stare
Jack knew she had witnessed it also.

"Junipero Serra is no hero," the girl bellowed. "No
more Euro-centric heroes! No more celebrating oppressive
regimes. Change the name! Change the name!"

The final three words became a chant. "Change the
name! Change the name!"

Just as protests elsewhere had demanded the destruction of recognition for George Washington and Thomas
Jefferson because they owned slaves, here the target was the
memory of the diminutive missionary.

"He enslaved Native Americans!" the purple-haired

leader cried, pointing to the statue of the saint. "He imposed his phony religion on their culture, and whipped them into submission. Tear it down! Tear it down!"

Sirens wailed in the distance.

"Let's get out of here," Jack said. "Must be a back way out of the parking lot."

Ropes snaked around the statue's neck and shoulders.

Gunning the engine, Jack managed to evade the rioters by driving toward the back of the administration hall. One of the "peaceful protestors" threw his skateboard at the rental car. It clanged on the trunk lid and bounced into the rose bushes.

"Jack," Bette said. "All those students. They were white. No black or brown skins anywhere."

"I know," Jack responded grimly. "I'm not even sure they *are* students. No classes meeting, right? And you know what else? Serra spent his life defending the natives from oppressive government regimes. If not for him," Jack offered as they turned onto a road leading out of the campus, "maybe there would truly have been slavery in California. But it's not about slavery, is it? It's anti-God and anti-America—which makes it anti-Israel too."

The sounds were off key, and not keeping time, but even so the amplified words of the rioters' chants reached them: Students are freedom fighters, learning how to fight. We're going to fight all day and night until we get this right. What side are you on? What side are you on? Peaceful Monterey echoed with cheering as the statue of Junipero Serra crashed from its pedestal.

"Can you imagine trying to reason with them?" Jack remarked grimly.

"Not when that—that thing—is there too," Bette returned with a shudder. "Name of Jesus, keep us safe from evil!"

"Sorry about Cannery Row," Jack apologized. "Maybe on the way back. How do you feel about Salinas? Steinbeck hung out there some too."

✧ ✧ ✧

Brahim Rahman was glad he had pretended his internet service was bad. Only the telephonic portion of his call to the New York headquarters of his boss was working, Rahman said. Listening to condemnation by voice was bad enough without seeing a disapproving face.

"You have been a very long time reporting," Bone Box said. "And even now you are not calling to report success, are you?"

Glancing out of the suite's bedroom toward where Tiny and Glen slouched on a couch, Rahman shook his head, forgetting the gesture could not be seen by phone. Glen had a black eye. Tiny, despite his immense size, had been knocked to the ground in the Pico riot. His face still carried the marks of being battered by skateboard deck edges and wheels.

"Well?" came the distant demand. "It is a poor workman who blames his tools."

Without pausing to wonder how Bone Box knew what he had been about to say, Rahman replied, "There has been no time to locate replacements. I will carry on and I will succeed—at least as far as Garrison and the Jewish woman are concerned."

"I already know you let the reporter escape." The flatness with which these words were uttered terrified Rahman. "She is already in Israel, under the protection of the IDF. She is no longer your concern."

"But the information she...."

"No longer your concern," Bone Box emphasized. "She will be discredited; that is all you need to know. As to the other two...."

"Yes?" Rahman asked eagerly; perhaps too eagerly.

"Even though you could not keep track of them, a helpful member of the U.S. State Department has done so for you. They are on their way to meet with fellows of the Hoover Institution in Palo Alto, California. They will be there later today or tomorrow morning." After a long pause, the expressionless voice continued, "It is now a matter of using them to remind others whose loyalty to us might be wavering what their fates will be if they defect. Do I make myself clear?"

"Hoover Institution."

"Do not fail me again, Rahman," the financial backer of the destruction of America warned. "I had such hopes for you."

Before Rahman could utter a single word of reassurance the line clicked dead.

NEW FACES, OLD DEMONS

It was just after sunset when, mandatory masks in place, Jack and Bette entered the Walmart store in Salinas. The aisles were packed with shoppers. A flood of customers of all ethnicities—black, white, Mexican, Asian—poured through the doors. They hailed one another with familiarity. It was clear that they were smiling behind their anti-virus masks.

Bette said, "They all know one another!"

"Salinas is a small town," Jack replied.

The festive atmosphere had the feel of a celebration about to break loose.

And so it did.

From the aisle leading to the bicycle display, an enormous black man climbed a ladder. He was wearing a blue-and-gold football jersey emblazoned with his name, SHARP.

"Jack!" Bette exclaimed with excitement. "It's Pastor Sharp. Shalom, Pastor!"

"Shalom!" Sharp responded. "Hey, Bette. Hey, Jack. Welcome!" He cupped his hands around his mouth and called, "Attention! Attention, y'all! You all know my name! Hallelujah! I'm Pastor Mike Sharp from Gospel Holiness Congregation. We have all been told not only is there no football for me to coach, but the governor says we can't worship in our church, or sing praises to the Lord in our church building! But, hey! There's no restriction for gathering or shopping or singing and praising God in Walmart! So here we are!"

A rousing cheer rose from every corner of the store. Shoppers abandoned carts and pushed forward toward the pastor who towered above them on the ladder.

People shouted, "Hallelujah! Hallelujah! Pastor Sharpe!"

"We are here!"

"The Holy Spirit is in this place!"

"We don't need a building!"

"We are the church! We are the church!"

"Hallelujah!"

"Revive us again, O Lord!"

"Take back America! Take back our land!"

"Come, Lord Jesus!"

Bette and Jack stood rooted in amazement beside the rack of Monterey Bay logo tee-shirts as hundreds more Christians, as if at a signal, suddenly burst through the doors and packed the store.

Pastor Mike raised one arm high and began to sing in a deep resonant voice that echoed from the far corners of Walmart!

"I raise a hallelujah! In the presence of my enemies!"

Four others stepped forward and joined with him, "We raise a hallelujah! Louder than the unbelief!"

The choir of five became a choir of twenty! Then a soaring flash mob of one hundred sang with power, declaring that their melody was the weapon which called heaven's power down to fight.

"Angels come to fight for me!"

Soon the holy melody was on the lips of everyone in the store. Bette and Jack held one another and sang with the crowd.

Security guards, floor managers, and checkout clerks joined countless customers!

"Up from the ashes hope will arise!"

Phones whipped out to record the miracle of the living church declaring to all of Salinas that Jesus Christ is Lord! There were perhaps two thousand in the congregation who worshipped through song for an hour. Then Pastor Mike, still perched on a step ladder, began to preach a powerful sermon from the book of Acts.

"When the day of Pentecost had fully come, they were all in one place *with one accord*!' And here we are: altogether, with one view in mind. One accord!" He continued, over the sound of cheers: "Suddenly a sound like the blowing of a violent wind came from heaven and filled the whole house where they were sitting. They saw what seemed to be tongues of fire that separated and came to rest on each one of them. All of them were filled with the Holy Spirit and began to speak in other tongues as the Spirit gave them utterance. And do you know what the Apostle Peter said would happen in the last days?"

"Tell us, pastor!"

"Peter quoted the Hebrew Prophet Joel: 'I will pour out my spirit on all people. Your sons and daughters will prophesy. Your old men will dream dreams. Your young men will see visions.' Now he spoke those words about that very first Day of Pentecost. If he called that celebration of the coming of the Holy Spirit, 'the last days'—where are we now?"

"The last days!" was shouted back at him.

As the preacher and the crowd cried out, Jack clasped Bette's hand tightly. From the corner of his eye, standing at his right, he saw four tall figures in white who were bathed in light.

"Jack! Do you see them?" Bette breathed in wonder.

"Yes!" Jack replied.

"Four of them," she cried! "Angels! Jack! In Walmart!" She laughed, and then pointed. "No! Look! There are five!"

At her proclamation, Eliyahu stepped from among the bright beings and motioned for Jack and Bette to follow him. With the preacher's voice echoing, and then fading behind them, Jack and Bette stepped over a threshold into the starry night.

✿ ✿ ✿

Bette and Jack saw themselves standing before a large, frosted glass door. Vague, diffused light penetrated through the glass panels. Occasionally the light brightened, then dimmed, as if concealing lightning flashes.

The door was sealed shut.

At a gesture from Eliyahu, both Bette and Jack bowed their heads. Immediately Jack sensed a clinging warmth that slowly spread from the crown of his head downwards.

It was the sensation of being anointed with oil—holy oil. Jack smiled and cried at the same time. He saw that Bette was doing the same; overwhelmed by the majesty of the moment.

A shared nod, and then Bette and Jack raised their hands, palms outward, toward the door—which shattered! In an instant the barrier was down, revealing that they stood on a high mountain. Overhead and all around were storm clouds, roiling with thunder and lightning. Still, supernatural peace surrounded them, filled them, and drew them forward.

Jack heard Bette singing and shouting in a language he had never heard before, then recognized he was doing the same thing at the same time. A beautiful harmony filled the space, and though the words were unknown the meaning was precise and powerful: "You, O Lord, are Holy and greatly to be praised! We lift our hearts to You, mighty King, as we sing the unending hymn of praise: 'Holy, Holy, Holy! Lord God of Hosts! Heaven and earth are full of Your glory. Hosanna in the highest!'"

From the furthest distance that they could see, at the furthest edge of the dark cloud, another light appeared that was not a flash of lightning. At first it appeared to be a fire-fly dancing toward them, as if on a gossamer thread. Then as the gleam approached, it resolved into a galloping white horse of immense size and unearthly beauty, that appeared to have wings.

In the next instant, just as the horse swept upon them,

Jack realized there was an angel mounted on the horse, and it was the angel's wings he had misunderstood. There was only a momentary flash to correct this perception and the mounted messenger thundered by. As he did so, Bette and Jack reached up, and both were swept aboard the horse's back.

Now they were galloping down from a high mountain peak at breakneck speed. There was a sense of incredible momentum, but no fear; no distress as they swept around curves and plunged down intervening ravines before the next vista appeared before them.

Halfway down the mountain—if such an immense height could be accurately divided into parts—the angel spoke a word of command. The horse stopped without flurry on the edge of a great precipice. Far below them lay a great valley, thickly carpeted with people—expectant peo-ple—watchful people—eager people.

"Come up!" Jack urged, waving to the crowd.

"Follow us!" Bette shouted. "He is almost here! The King is coming! Come and greet Him!"

Now atop the mount that had been shrouded in dark-ness was a glowing sphere. *I've seen this before,* Jack realized. *It's the Shekinah glory of the Lord.*

Bette spoke to Jack without even moving her lips. "We are to lead them to the very presence of the Lord, Jack," she said. "It is now. It is time. It is us. And it is for each of them to bring others with them."

And in that fragment of time mountain and glory, horse

and rider, multitude of people, disappeared—replaced by the fluorescent-bulb-lit interior of the Salinas Walmart.

But there was still an echo of thunder and summons in the hymns of praise.

12

EARS TO LISTEN, EYES TO SEE

The two-hundred-eighty-five-foot tall Hoover Tower pinned Palo Alto, California, to the San Francisco Peninsula. Perhaps the imposing pillar was the only thing keeping the bay from widening, and the City of San Francisco from floating off, out into the Pacific Ocean, far, far to the left of the rest of the United States.

Beginning life just after the First World War as the 'Hoover Library on War,' the original establishing fund was donated by Stanford alum Herbert Hoover before he became the U.S. president. This political and economic think-tank associated with Stanford University now sported the imposing title: 'Hoover Institution on War, Revolution and Peace.'

The scholarly consortium attracted leading thinkers and

policy-makers because of its dedication to private enterprise, personal rights, and the American system. Among its
distinguished fellows were warfare and revolution scholar
Victor Davis Hanson, economics maven Thomas Sowell,
and race relations expert Shelby Steele.

After checking in and receiving their visitor badges,
Bette and Jack were escorted to the conference room and
offered a choice of coffee or juice. Both declined, but
accepted bottled water. The expansive golden birch conference table that seated twenty-five, the thickly carpeted floor,
and the windowless, soundproof space conveyed a sense of
gravity and foreboding.

Jack muttered to Bette. "The brain power in this place
is a couple orders of magnitude past mine. Maybe we
should just sneak out now."

"What are you whispering?" Bette demanded.
"You have advised European governments about the
Middle East...."

Jack replied. "I didn't give them the answers they
wanted about how nasty, terrible, and awful Israel is."

Speaking over the top of Jack's plaintive joke, Bette said,
"And Bibi Netanyahu asked for you personally." She ignored
Jack's outburst of humility. "Besides," she said, quoting the
Lord God, as recorded by the prophet Jeremiah: "'I know
the plans I have for you, says the Lord; plans for your welfare
and not for evil; to give you a future and a hope.' So you see,
Jack, you are here because God wants you here."

When the door opened and a pair of Hoover Institution

fellows entered, all Jack's nervousness evaporated. "Caroline!" he greeted the diminutive, olive-skinned beauty who led the group into the room. "How wonderful to see you again! Bette, this is Caroline da Souza from Lisbon, Portugal. She is an expert on Middle Eastern affairs who attended meetings with me in London."

"Butted heads with you, you mean," Caroline returned. "Very pleased to meet you, Mrs. Garrison. Jack and I were on opposite sides of many things regarding Israel, but it seems he has come to his senses at last. Thanks to you, no doubt. Mazel tov! I hear you two were recently married."

"So recently that I'm still adjusting to being called Mrs. Garrison," Bette replied. "Please call me Bette."

"And I am Caroline. Now let me complete the introductions."

The other member of the institution's committee was a tall, slender woman with coffee-colored skin. Her eyes were serious. She had a haunted quality, Jack thought, possibly related to the jagged scar that marred her otherwise flawlessly smooth cheek.

"This is Hani Aden," Caroline said. "Our newest fellow. Like another Hoover fellow, and Hani's fellow countrywoman, Ayaan Hirsi Ali, Hani is from Somalia. She is also a tireless advocate for religious freedom, and women's rights, with a death threat hanging over her head."

"*Shalom aleicum,*" Hani offered.

"*Aleicum shalom,*" Bette and Jack returned. "But you are not Jewish?" Bette queried.

"No," Hani returned. "Born and raised Muslim, but now a Christian."

"Please, let's sit," Caroline urged, acting the part of host.

"But you, I think, are Jewish?" Bette continued, directing the question toward Caroline and receiving a nodding smile in return. "Da Souza is Portuguese, but you are of Sephardic heritage? I guessed because I have da Souza cousins, and you look like family."

"My distant ancestor—Rodrigo da Souza—was one of a handful of Jews who came to the Americas with Columbus," Caroline agreed. "Perhaps that is what drew me here to the U.S. And now I think we should begin exploring the reason for this gathering."

"Exactly," Jack concurred. "Why are we here? We're already in America at the request of the Israeli diplomatic service. Bette and I were asked by the Israeli consulate to come here today. Trump's Deal of the Century—the Abrahamic Accord peace treaty between Israel and the UAE—has been signed. With God's help, Trump has done the impossible. For the first time in thousands of years, the brothers of common blood— nations which are descendants of Abraham—have joined together in a pact to protect one another from a common enemy. It is the fulfillment of biblical prophecy unlike any the world has ever seen."

After a glance at both Hani, Caroline opened the discussion. "This is a critical period in U.S.—Middle East relations and peace between Israel and others in the region. Shiite Iran wants to reestablish a Persian Empire. Iran has support from China. Turkey, as a Sunni Muslim state, is in opposition to Shiite Iran. Turkey believes Saudi Arabia is getting too comfortable with Israel. Turkey's Erdogan is moving away from a secular nation toward being a hardline Sunni state. Russian support for the Syrian regime is coupled with Russian ambitions in the region. At the moment Turkey has sided with the U.S. and against Russia in Libya, for example."

Jack interjected, "The Turks are not a nation related to Abraham. Erdogan has turned the Hagia Sophia— once the mother church of all Christianity—back into a mosque."

Caroline agreed. "The Ottomans captured Constantinople hundreds of years ago. The Hagia Sophia was a church, then a mosque, then a museum, now it's a mosque again."

Hani added, "Erdogan is flexing Turkey's muscles to be recognized as an Islamic champion. So he is currying favor with Sunni extremists in Iran. He is playing games with the U.S. about fending off Russian advances in the region, while always pushing the line to see where the West will react. Hagia Sophia is one more such provocation."

"And what about Israel?" Bette queried. "I know about Iranian-backed terrorists, but I know very little about Turkey. How can we help?"

Hani elaborated on the purpose of the meeting. "We need a—how shall I put this? A detailed biblical perspective."

All eyes turned toward Jack.

Jack hesitated a moment, then opened his brief case, pulling out a sheaf of hand written notes on a lined yellow pad, and a well-worn Bible.

"Alright then, here it is. Everything we see happening in Israel today is a fulfillment of biblical prophecy. The Abrahamic Accord between Israel and the United Arab Emirates; what does this mean? And so, I am going to be using my notes. I want to go through it a little quickly, but I want to paint a picture for you because Bible prophecy is happening now; its unfolding now. And I am telling you it is time to wake up, and look up, and get ready for the coming of the Lord."

Caroline closed her eyes then asked, "We are all Christians here. Would you mind if we open with prayer?"

Each of the scholars bowed their heads as Jack prayed, *"Heavenly Father, we welcome the Holy Spirit. And I pray that you will take now, these scriptures, and as we lay them out and lay a foundation, and Lord put them one upon the other. I pray that those who hear this message, God your spirit will press and impress the truth like a seed planted within their heart. Open eyes to see what is happening, that your word is coming to pass for such a time as this. And Lord that it will ignite a fire and a flame within our heart to live our lives with passion, with boldness, to love you, to follow you, and to share our faith, and to bring our family and our friends into a personal relationship with Jesus Christ. We ask all these things in the mighty, worthy name of Jesus. Amen."*

Hani asked, "So, Jack, where is this moment in scripture?

There has been an announcement about this historic peace accord. This is only the third Muslim nation that has ever made a peace deal with Israel. We remember in history, a while ago, that Israel made peace with Egypt, and then later they made peace with Jordan, but it has been at a stalemate for a long time. Now there is something going on, something is brewing, even bigger than this."

Jack replied, "I believe this is no little thing; not just a tentative beginning. This announcement of a brand new, historic, peace agreement between Israel and the United Arab Emirates is a major turning point in world history."

Caroline asked, "Do you believe that prophecy gives us the headlines of tomorrow?"

Jack answered, "We as believers have inside information. I believe that the American President is a modern day Cyrus. He established Jerusalem as the capital of Israel. He will take part in the rebuilding of a Jewish Temple. And I am going to share with you some of the prophecies from the Prophet Daniel that are two thousand five hundred years old. So the Bible tells us what is happening. The Bible tells us where it is going to happen. And the Bible tells us how it is going to happen in this prophetic season in which we are living. So, I want to say, we must look at all the events happening in the world through the lens of scripture, because scripture interprets scripture, line upon line, precept upon precept. We have got to go through the lens of biblical prophecy."

Bette encouraged Jack, "So where should we look first?"

Jack flipped through his notes, then opened his Bible. "Let's look at the book of Daniel, chapter nine, verse twenty-seven, because this is what is happening right now. It says, "then he shall confirm a covenant with many for one week", and I believe the "he" there is the Antichrist. The reference to a week means seven years."

Hani scribbled notes as Jack spoke. "So what this says is: at the end of days Israel's re-gathered. This began in 1948. They have trouble with all their neighbors. The Middle East is in crisis, and there is a need for a covenant of peace. Literally a covenant of land for peace, and the Antichrist who will come later in the timeline, will be involved in what the Bible calls 'the end of days.'"

Jack confirmed her statement. "Yes. So 'he shall confirm a covenant with many' for one week—seven years. But in the middle of the week—that means after three and a half years—'He shall bring an end to sacrifice and offering. And on the wing of abominations shall be one who makes desolate, even until the consummation, which is determined, is poured out on the desolate.'"

Hani stared at the notes with a puzzled look. "I'm not sure I follow."

Jack explained, "So not only does the Bible say there will be a need to be a peace deal in the last days between Israel and her neighbors, land for peace, but there will also be one who confirms that covenant. And there must clearly a Jewish temple that is rebuilt on the Temple Mount where they began initiating sacrifices. As a matter of fact, I believe

Jerusalem will finally recognize the original United Nations mandate that the Temple Mount should be open to all three monotheistic faiths."

Pausing with a frown on his face, Jack resumed. "Then the Antichrist comes and stops that sacrifice in the middle of the week. That means after the first three and a half years. It is called the 70th week of Daniel. So, we should be expecting at this time that Daniel 9:27 would come to pass."

Caroline's serious expression brightened as the meaning of the prophecy began to make sense. "So, there will be a peace treaty that kind of falls apart? It will then need to be reconfirmed. And it is the Antichrist comes along in the end and confirms a treaty of peace between Israel and her neighbors."

Jack agreed. "What is interesting is in the Hebrew, where it says, 'he will confirm a covenant with many,' the Hebrew word for many, the root word in Hebrew, is *rab*.

"I believe the initial peace deal goes all the way back to the Oslo Peace Accords. If you will remember it was in the early 90's. 1993 to 1995, there was a peace deal, a peace treaty that was called the Oslo Peace Accords, and it was signed. And who was Israel's Prime Minister at that time? It was Prime Minister Rabin! Literally, the name of the Prime Minister is Rab, the root word for many! There will be a peace deal with many! Well, so that Oslo Accord came, and then of course, halfway through it fell apart. And Yasser Arafat and the Palestinians, you know, they protested, and they fought, and they did the intifada, and said no, they broke it up. It was happening but it failed, it fell apart."

Caroline reached for Jack's Bible. He grinned at her eagerness. She read in silence and then spoke. "So Daniel says they will be struggling toward a peace deal, and then he, the Antichrist, comes to confirm or strengthen the covenant that had already been started."

Hani asked, "Do you think the Anti-Christ is alive now?"

Jack nodded. "Waiting in the wings for men of faith, like Trump, to pass from center stage. Yes, I believe the Anti-Christ is alive now. When Trump is no longer in a position of world influence, the Anti-Christ will rise up, step in, and destroy all that is good." Jack nodded. "And I believe this all relates to that Deal of the Century that was presented by President Trump on January 28, 2020. He said we have a new peace deal that is coming, and now the United Arab Emirates, only the third Muslim country to want to enter into a peace deal with Israel, is coming to pass. Jews and Arabs, half brothers; the sons of Abraham. So, this is the hour the nations of the world are beginning to focus on Israel, because the United Arab Emirates is only the first. Other countries in the Middle East have said, 'we also want to enter into peace.' Other Sunni nations want to enter into a peace deal with Israel. Bahrain has said they want to look at a peace deal with Israel. They do not just want the United Arab Emirates to have it. Saudi Arabia said, down the road they would also be interested in a peace deal with Israel. Sudan said they want a peace deal with Israel."

Hani exclaimed, "Amazing! Unthinkable until President Trump!"

Caroline cried, "A peace deal with many! Started with the Oslo Accords. Clinton and with Prime Minister Rabin, but now it is moving into a new, higher gear."

Jack continued, "So, the foundation has been laid and I believe that what we are seeing now with the Abrahamic Accord is a powerful foundation. This is only the beginning of the fulfillment of the confirmation of the peace deal that Daniel 9:27 talked about."

Hani said, "I want to ask a question. Please explain what is motivating these Arab nations—to make peace with Israel *now*?"

Jack scanned his notes. "One of the things that came out of this new peace deal offered by the United Arab Emirates is they are sending a message. They are sending a message to the Palestinians. And they are basically saying look, yes, the Palestinians are our brothers, and we want for them to work out a peace deal with Israel. But we have been waiting. We have our own country. We have our own interests. We have our own reasons why we would like to normalize relations with Israel. Look, Israel has technology. They have medical research. They have protection that they can bring to us and so we have our own interests. We have waited for over seventy years and nothing has happened between Israel and you Palestinians. We are tired of waiting. So, I think it is a message that is being sent. And with other countries lining up behind the United Arab Emirates, it is signaling a sea change that is happening in the Middle East."

Hani asked, "Why is the United Arab Emirates saying this?"

Jack smiled. "Because they need Israel. Not only just with Israel, but the other Gulf nations, the Bible says, are going to come together. I believe these Gulf nations are going to be the many who will enter into this peace deal with Israel. They are being forced under the umbrella of protection with Israel. Why? Because they are Sunni nations, and many of those within them are also Arab."

Caroline cleared her throat then spoke. "You have the Shiites; the Shiites are Iran. They are the rejectionists. They are against peace. They are against Israel."

Jack added, "They are against the covenant. They are against any kind of a deal ever being made, even land for peace. So, what is interesting is that the Shiites literally are going towards a nuclear weapon and they are ready to use it."

Hani inquired, "I have asked this question before. If and when they get that bomb, who is the first one they would threaten to use it against? Who is the first country targeted?"

Jack replied, "Everybody thinks it's Israel. But no. Nor America. No. Who is number one nation that Shiite Iran would want to take over? Saudi Arabia! Because the

Shiites, who are only ten to fifteen per cent of the Muslim world, have a totally different theology than the Sunni Muslims. Therefore, they send terrorists into Saudi Arabia with drones to destroy the oil fields of Saudi Arabia."

Caroline pressed for clarification, "Is theology enough reason to make Saudi Arabia Iran's number one target?"

Jack explained, "Because Iran believes that their sect of Islam must take over the whole world. But how can you take over the whole world when within Islam over one and a half billion people are not united? So, their goal is first they must unite all of Islam under Shiite rule. Then they go after the little Satan: Israel. Then they go after the big Satan, which is America. So, in a sense the Gulf nations are feeling that little red laser light of the Shiite aggression; militias and terrorist groups. And they feel that pressure that Iran wants to take over. And they ask what can they do? Where can they go? And so, the Gulf nations are now looking to form an alliance with Israel."

Hani asked, "What's next?"

Jack answered, "Here is a beautiful thing: the Sunni nations, the Bible says, are going to embrace the American/Israeli peace agreement, because of the threat of Iran. Iran says no to Israel, no to peace, no to everything."

Caroline considered these facts. "Tell me again. How are the Arabs and Israel linked in biblical prophecy?"

Jack laughed with delight. "This is fascinating! Summing it up, the sons of Abraham are at last united. Remember this. Think of what Trump called the United Arab Emirates

peace accord with Israel? He called it the *Abrahamic Accord!*
The Sunni nations, the majority of them, are the seed of
Abraham. Some of them are the children of Abraham
through Ishmael. But some of them are the seed of
Abraham through, you remember that Sarah died, and
Abraham got remarried to a woman named Keturah, and
had sons and children and descendants. So those spread
out from all over the East. So literally when you look at
Abraham and his children it is not just between Ishmael who
came from Hagar, but it is Keturah and her children. These
are all that came all throughout that region of Arabia and
that part of the world within the Middle East. These are the
children of Abraham. They are related by blood to the Jews.
All of them trace their ancestry back to Abraham. And what
is interesting is they say, 'Hey, look. We need Israel. We need
their technology.' I mean Israel as a nation is like the Silicon
Valley of the whole Middle East and that part of the world,
they go we need that. There's medical research that can be
taken advantage of by many of these Gulf nations, and the
threat of Iran coming against them. So, they are saying,
'Israel has nuclear weapons; they could protect us. We could
come underneath the umbrella of Israel if we normalize
relations. If we wait for the Palestinian peace accord, it will
never happen.'

"And they are feeling the pressure," Jack amplified.
"They are feeling the threat. They are feeling, you know,
that they are losing time. And they have waited for seventy
years and nothing has moved forward. So, now they are

ready to move. They are ready to act; ready to normalize relations.

Bette remarked quietly, "It's all in Daniel."

Jack agreed, "Basically, the Bible laid this out. The Sunni nations will come into an embrace with Israel and even America and Trump's peace deal. And the Bible divides those who will embrace Israel, and bless Israel, and compromise with Israel, and make land for peace, on the one side. And those who are against Israel, reject Israel, like Iran—no land for peace, no compromise—and those two groups are planted right there in the Middle East. And they are going to arise, and there you have the basis of ultimately the battle of Armageddon between those two groups. So, there are the sheep nations that support Israel, and the goat nations that are against and opposed to Israel. Like King Cyrus of old, Trump knows the promise of Genesis 12:1-3. Trump, like American Presidents before him, has claimed the Cyrus Mandate that those who bless Israel will be blessed. But what I think is amazing is that God is using circumstances right now. He is moving the descendants of Abraham, that came through Keturah and through Hagar. He is moving them to their cousins, which are the Jewish people, the descendants of Abraham Isaac and Jacob. And so, they have blood, they share blood with one another. They are cousins to one another, it makes sense that they could come together mutual blessing, mutual protection, mutual economic and technology and medical benefit."

"They are family," Hani said in awe. "All descendants of Abraham."

Jack tapped his finger on the open Bible. "So that is what is happening in developing on the one side. On the other side is Iran; the rejectionists, and the Bible laid that out as well. So, where does the Bible speak of the Shiite rejection of Israel? In Daniel, chapter eleven, verse thirty-two, it says 'those who do wickedly against the covenant he shall corrupt with flattery; but the people who know their God shall be strong, and carry out great exploits'. Basically, this says that there will be those nations that will go with Israel, and go with the peace deal, there will be those who fight it, which I believe is Iran's Shiite rejection. They share no blood with the Arab people. There is no bloodline connecting the Iranian Shiites to Abraham. Iran is the Persia of the Bible. They are not related to those who are the descendants of Abraham. But the Sunnis, many of them Arabs, that come from Abraham, share blood with Israel. So, God is using geopolitical circumstances to force and compel for practical reasons, pragmatic reasons, economic reasons, protection reasons, all of these things. He's bringing the Abrahamic family together. This is the wisdom of God, the sovereignty of God, the plan of God that is working all these things.

"So, look, this is where we are at. It has landed. It has arrived. We are not going back. There is no new normal. We are heading into exactly what Jesus described in Matthew 24: pandemics followed by pandemics, nation against nation, kingdom against kingdom. In the Greek, that's *ethnos* versus *ethnos*, which means ethnicity against ethnicity. There is going to be racial tension. Jesus said it is one of the signs of the end times. We are seeing it now. We are coming to a point of global crisis. And now as this pandemic continues to move forward and screech the economies to halt, the global economy is headed towards a collapse. Global leaders say it is headed towards a reset, which means a collapse, where you have to start all over again. And this is exactly what the Bible said the scenario would be in the end days."

Caroline asked, "Jack? You believe we are in those days—now?"

Jack nodded gravely. "If not already in them, that at the very edge."

Hani said quietly to Bette, "You are *sabra.* Born in Israel and a Jewish believer in Yeshua. How do you respond to all this? How do you summarize it?"

Bette paused, choosing her words carefully. "In the heart of every Jew," she said, "Are the tears of Abraham, weeping for Ishmael. We are witnessing the fulfillment of that longing *right now.* "

13

No Weapon Forged....

It was with the total sense of 'mission accomplished' that Bette and Jack left the bay area to head back to L.A. There would be a report to deliver to Morrie Ryskind at the Israeli Consulate, but given this morning's news, both knew it was already overshadowed.

President Trump had already delivered on the Abraham Accord! The United Arab Emirates would soon normalize relations with Israel, becoming just the third Arab nation—following Egypt and Jordan—to do so. Other moderate Arab nations quickly made overtures of peace: Bahrain. Oman. Maybe a distant Mediterranean nation like Morocco would likewise follow suit.

What had Pastor Sharp said about the first Day of Pentecost? *They were all together in one accord?* There was something supernaturally brilliant about reconciling the branches of Abraham's descendants. Even if this was just a hesitant first step, it truly was the "Deal of the Century."

What was more, it left the hard-line Muslim nations like Iran—who were not even offspring of Ishmael, and therefore *not* related to Abraham—on the outside, looking in. The Palestinians were predictably not happy. The new deal did put Israeli annexation of more territory on hold; but did not reject it forever. The Accord caused a temporary breathing space for the whole region.

Suiting actions to thoughts, Jack drew a deep breath and let it out slowly. "You know," he said to Bette. "Maybe now we can actually just relax for a few days. No more international chores. No more visions."

"No more bad guys," Bette returned. "A real honeymoon at last before we head back to Israel."

"Great idea!" Jack replied as he wheeled their rental car around a curve and onto the concrete-arch span of the Bixby Canyon Bridge; the northern gateway to Big Sur. "Keep feasting your eyes while I watch the road," he advised. "The best of the Cali-coast scenery is from here south. Carmel to Ragged Point, here we come."

There was a delicious sense of no pressure and no worries. They stopped for coffee. They turned off Highway 1 to climb still higher up the cliff face and visit the New Camaldoli Monastery, for no more reason than Bette had remarked, "There is a monastery here? I had no idea."

Though no service was in progress, they entered the

simple chapel with a feeling of hushed reverence. The day-light streaming in from the peak of the sanctuary embraced the wooden-paneled ceiling—and Jack and Bette—with God's presence. "Jesus, I trust in You," Jack whispered.

"Jesus, I love You," Bette added.

Back on the road again, this stretch of the Pacific Coast Highway clung to the Santa Lucia Mountains above a nearly sheer drop to the Pacific like a thin cobweb barely anchored to a curtain rod. "Is this scary for you, Jack?" Bette asked.

"Not me," Jack returned. "I've got my eyes closed."

That remark earned him a carefully restrained tap on the head.

"Another idea," Jack said. "While we *could* make it all the way back to the place we stayed near Pismo Beach—or even further south—but why? Why don't we stay where we have all the world spread out at our feet?"

"You wouldn't suggest that notion without already hav-ing something in mind."

"Indeed, beautiful lady. Ragged Point. Almost, but not quite where this road comes back to earth again. Besides, then tomorrow we can see if Hearst Castle is open for visi-tors, or hang out in a little place called Cambria; artsy-craftsy shops and wine-tasting."

"Jack," Bette said, hugging his arm with delight. "Anything you say."

With about ten miles still to go to reach Ragged Point, and no one approaching northward along the highway in several minutes, Jack was not at all concerned when a large pickup truck appeared in his mirror. The Ford F-250 roared up behind them, going at least twenty miles an hour faster than Jack's moderate pace.

"That guy is in way too big a hurry for this road," Jack said. "Soon as there's a place I'll let him by."

That was the issue: there was no place to pull over. On the right hand margin there was a sheer drop of a couple hundred feet.

The overtaking truck crept to within a couple feet of Jack's rear bumper. "Jack," Bette warned. "The guy hanging out the passenger window? I think he's the giant thug we saw on Pico in L.A. when they were trying to kill Tabitha. Now they're after us again."

Jack was barely keeping ahead of the pursuing truck, tires squealing around blind curves. His white-knuckled grip betrayed the tension of looking for a place to get out of the way—and finding none. The Ford roared up again on a straight stretch and tapped Jack's bumper. Only by seeing it about to happen and pressing the accelerator pedal was Jack able to keep control.

The killers changed tactics.

The Ford roared up alongside Jack and Bette and made a move to force them over the edge.

"Can't stop!" Jack said through gritted teeth. "They have guns too."

When Jack slowed, so did the Ford. When he tried to shoot through the gap, the assailants sped up again. Once they barely missed colliding after the Ford swerved into his barely-vacated space. Spinning the wheel, Jack shot around them into the on-coming lane, then back.

This could not go on. Something had to break soon.

As if sensing Jack's weariness, attackers closed in again, driving on the wrong side of the road and preparing for the final blow.

Just before it came, Jack stomped the brakes hard and swerved again into the opposite lane; found he was facing an on-coming SUV. Another abrupt jerk of the steering wheel, accompanied by Bette's scream, brought them into a drainage ditch, where the engine died.

The approaching SUV had turned the opposite way. Striking the Ford on the left front fender, the combined impact caused the killers' truck to dangle over the Pacific— but only for a moment. There was a frantic scrabbling noise as the two would-be assassins tried to free jammed doors—and then the Ford toppled sideways and plunged onto the rocks and onto the waves that lapping one hundred-fifty feet below.

The SUV had stopped safely. The driver backed out of the wrong lane to pull up next to Jack and Bette.

"Bette! Bette!" Jack said urgently. "Are you okay?"

Both doors of the SUV opened.

"I think so," she replied, just as someone with Middle Eastern features and black hair tapped on her window.

"Jack!" Bette shrieked. "From L.A. The man with the cell phone who was watching us!"

"Are you all right, Mister and Missus Garrison? I'm Avi, from the consulate. Good thing we put that tracking fob on your key chain. You've been terribly hard to keep up with. Our men in Paris said they couldn't manage to stay with you at all!"

✡ ✡ ✡

Bette was too emotionally drained to stay awake, but the effect on Jack was just the opposite. His adrenalin still raging, he was too keyed up to sleep.

The night after the harrowing Highway 1 escape was also the night of the full moon. The silvery orb was still hidden behind an obscuring wall of hills and peaks, but already it outlined them with a gleaming border. As Jack watched, the lunar body climbed still higher until it peeked over the rim of the coast range. The first of the unbound rays penetrated the darkness of the shore, and impaled the placid ocean with a spear of light.

It was also the last full moon before *Rosh Hoshana,* Jack mused. In two weeks would come the new moon, the Feast of Trumpets, the Jewish New Year, and the start of the Ten Days of Awe, leading to the Day of Atonement.

What a time, Jack thought. *If ever the entire world needed repentance leading to atonement, this is it. There certainly is "pestilence among the people."*

"*If my people, who are called by My Name—*" Jack quoted the rest of God's Second Chronicles 7 promise to himself, while shaking his head and then muttering, "'will humble themselves, and pray, and seek My face....'

"A mighty big set of 'ifs,' Lord. People don't spend a lot of time 'turning from their wicked ways' these days. Or if they do, they've probably already done it. And the people who really should be horrified of the burden of their sin have no conscience about it at all. Can't you terrify them, Lord? I don't ask You to destroy them. Just wake them up! The pro-abortion crowd. The there-is-no-God folks. Give them frightening dreams that will once and for all make them really seek You."

What was that discussion Jack dimly recalled from a long ago visit with his dear friend, Lev? "Contrary to what the devil wants people to believe about God, people choose to go to hell of their own free will. God doesn't want to send anyone there, but humans die every day having chosen against letting Jesus into their lives."

Bette was fast asleep, but Jack continued praying over their life together and this mission from Israel to the United States. Had they made any progress toward the goal of waking up American Christians to the danger they faced? Was 'the end of the age' truly in sight, and would Yeshua Messiah truly be returning soon?

Turning away from the balcony Jack reseated himself on the sofa in the front room of the hotel suite. Since the resort was west of the bay and their window faced the east, Jack was able to continuing watching the moon rise as it stretched and grew, flooding earth and sea with a blaze of light.

The moon continued to grow as it rode aloft until it seemed to fill the entire horizon from north to south. *It's a vision,* Jack realized. *Or a dream.*

Suddenly it was blinding. Jack blinked away tears and tried to tear himself away from staring, but he could not break eye contact with something that was now much brighter than—much more important than—just the moon.

I am seeing the Glory of God. The Shekinah!

A sudden draft of warm air floated around Jack's face. The moist coolness of the ocean breeze was gone.

It's not the moon, Jack realized. *It's a candle flame. No, it's not just a single candle. It's a menorah. I'm seeing a seven-branched candlestick, like in the Temple.*

At the center of the converging, overlapping, and waving flames stood a man. *It's Jesus,* Jack knew with a rush of comprehension. *I'm seeing Jesus in the Shekinah light of a heavenly menorah.*

Then Jack saw himself as if from a distance. He was no longer seated in a hotel room but standing on a platform, speaking to thousands of people. Jack was not speaking about himself nor were the words he spoke coming from his own thoughts. A voice whispered to him, "When they bring you before the authorities, do not worry about how or what you should answer, or what you should say, for the Holy Spirit will teach you in that very hour what you ought to say."

The all-powerful, all-embracing light of Jesus streamed over Jack's shoulders and out to the audience. The one delivering the message was Jack, but the message *was* Jesus! People were praying and shouting and worshipping and singing and praying, all at the same time—and it was a beautiful harmony of sound.

In the next moment the melody was shattered by a trumpet blast—a host of trumpets—a thousand ram's horn shofars, all blaring at once! It was a signal.

Jack heard the rushing of wings like a mighty wind. Thousands and thousands of angels were dispatched from behind the menorah to fan out in all directions across the sky toward every part of the earth.

Jack knew—somehow completely knew—that every angelic messenger had been charged with a special mission, and each was eager to carry out his assignment.

Heaven is on the move! Jack thought. *Get ready! The King is Coming!*

Jack was once again on the sofa in the hotel suite, but he did not remain there long. Grabbing his Bible from the table he thumbed it eagerly until he found what he sought in the book of Revelations. "Bette," he called urgently. "Bette, wake up and listen to this: 'And I saw seven golden lampstands, and in the midst of the seven lampstands One like the Son of Man! He's coming! He's truly coming soon!"

EPILOGUE

The Feast of Trumpets arrived in the land of Israel.

Would it be the last before the return of Yeshua HaMashiach?
Jack wondered, as the sun sank low in the western sky.

President Trump's 'Abrahamic Accord' between Israel and the United Arab Emirates was a fulfillment of biblical prophecy. There was very little left to be completed on the world stage.

President Trump and the United States had once again fulfilled the Cyrus Mandate on behalf of Israel—reconciling, as between cousins, the descendants of Abraham's sons Isaac and Ishmael.

It was a masterful stroke.

Bette prepared a feast in Dodi's kitchen for a handful of guests. A long table was set in Dodi's courtyard. Though she could not see the details, she directed the scene-setting, down to the color of flowers in the center pieces.

Lon Silver and his wife arrived with Bette's brother, Benni, and a dozen bottles of their finest wine as an offering. Benni carried his curved kudu-horn shofar. Lev and Katy arrived with their pack of chattering children, and enough dessert to feed everyone and several dozen more.

Last to arrive to the celebration was Tabitha Vanderhorst and her handsome, plain-clothes IDF bodyguard. Jack spotted the bulge of a sidearm in the guard's shoulder holster.

Tabitha's hair was cut short and dyed a coppery red. Her name had been changed. After a crash course in Hebrew, she was protected and secure in her new identity, living in an apartment near the King David Hotel.

The details she provided of corruption and the outside influence on the American media and leftist politicians by China, Russia and the Deep State Globalists had been verified.

Meanwhile, the Abraham Accord was announced. The children of Isaac and Ishmael had come to terms. Israel flew the flag of the United Arab Emirates as the terms of President Trump's brokered peace agreement between the UAE and Israel were released. The Israeli flag was projected on the tallest skyscraper in Dubai, UAE Ambassadors would soon be exchanged.

Normal diplomatic relations for the first time ever.

As Trump had predicted, the Palestinians had refused to

cooperate with the original peace proposal, so Israel and the UAE, with guidance from the American government, had simply struck a deal without them.

Both Israel and the U.S. indicated that the annexation of Judea and Samaria by Israel was not canceled, but only delayed.

It was suspected that the explosion which leveled Beirut, only days before the Abraham Accord was announced, was Iran's reply to any peace in the Middle East not imposed by them.

Behind the high walls of Dodi's refuge, the masks were removed and apprehension melted away. Laughter and light-hearted banter replaced all grim conversation about political chaos, threats, and plagues.

The table glistened with silver and crystal goblets and blue floral Meissen china on white linen.

Candles were lit and prayers were recited by Lon as the sun melted like molten gold. The air was suddenly filled with the blasts of countless shofars announcing the Glory of Almighty God. Benni raised the shofar to his lips and joined the chorus. All of Jerusalem, for one glorious hour, shone in variegated gold.

Dodi was seated like a queen at the head of her table. She instructed that Tabitha Vanderhorst must sit at her right hand.

With a regal wave she instructed, "Bette, please, if you will, go fetch the basket for Tabitha, the newest member of the family of Israel.

Bette nudged Jack and hurried into the house. In a moment she returned as Dodi addressed Tabitha. "Tabitha, you are courageous woman, a woman of valor. No doubt you risked your life to provide truth about the bad actors in the world to the Israeli and American governments. Bette and Jack have told me about the terrible night that you escaped what was surely intended to be your death."

Tabitha touched Dodi's hand in response. "What would have happened without Jack and Bette? I don't know. A very dangerous night."

Dodi squeezed Tabitha's fingers. "And what did you return home to fetch?"

Tabitha looked down. "Oh. Oh I didn't want to bring anything. Nothing but…." She glanced at Bette helplessly. "I just wanted to bring my kitty with me. Harpo."

"Ah, yes. I'm so sorry. I hated to hear what happened to your dear Harpo." Dodi motioned for Bette to bring the picnic basket. "And so, my dear, I sent Bette and Jack on a quest to find the perfect gift for you." Dodi smiled gently. "You may give it to our dear Tabitha now, please."

Bette place the basket in Tabitha's lap. "Open it. Go ahead."

Tabitha stared at the wicker container as a soft mewing sound escaped. In awe, she opened the lid and gasped, "What is this?" she cried out with joy.

All at the table cheered, as in the distance shofars echoed through the city.

A tiny yellow kitten with wide blue eyes blinked up at

her. She scooped him up and nuzzled him. "Oh, look at
you! Look at you!" Tears streamed down Tabitha's cheeks.
Instantly the kitten began to purr.

Dodi laughed, "He is a Jerusalem kitten. Born free. Of
independent mind, but very brave and loyal. These wild
cats chase after anything that tweets. They tell me with the
color of his yellow fur, he bears a resemblance to a certain
fellow in the news. I hope you don't mind, but, after all, it is
Feast of Trumpets. So, I have named your little wildcat for
you: Trumpet."

Laughter erupted and all raised their glasses in a
toast. Jack declared, "And it was written: they were all of
one accord!"

AN OPEN INVITATION

If you would like to take the step that will connect you with Yeshus—Jesus the Messiah—consider this:

Jesus came from heaven to show us "the Way, the Truth, and the Life." (John 14:6) He died on the cross for our sins and rose from the dead on the third day. He says, "Behold, I stand at the door and knock, and if any man hears my voice, and opens the door, I will come in to him, and sup with him, and he with me." (Rev. 3:20)

You can have a personal relationship with God through Jesus Christ. In a simple prayer, tell Him you know you are a sinner, and ask forgiveness. Tell Him you believe He died for your sins, rose from the dead, and you want to invite Him to come into your heart. Tell Him you want to follow Him as your personal Lord and Savior, in His Name.

And if you would like more information on how to grow spiritually, please visit *www.raybentley.com*

ABOUT THE AUTHORS

 RAY BENTLEY is a pastor, prophecy expert, and author. He founded Maranatha Chapel in August 1984. Today Maranatha serves 7,000 people weekly. His daily radio show can be heard across the United States and around the world. A variety of printed, audio, and video resources for study can be found at maranatha. tv and RayBentley.com. Ray has authored nine books, including The Elijah Chronicles: *On the Mountain of the Lord*, *The Threshing Floor*, and *The Cyrus Mandate*. Ray and his wife, Vicki, have two grown children and seven grandchildren.

 BODIE THOENE with her husband and writing partner Brock, has written over seventy works of historical fiction. Over 35 million of these best selling novels are in print in thirty languages. Her byline has appeared in prestigious periodicals such as *U.S. News & World Report*, *The American West*, and *The Saturday Evening Post*. She also worked for John Wayne's Batjac Productions and ABC Circle Films as a writer and researcher. John Wayne described her as a writer with talent that captures the people and the times. She has degrees in journalism and communications. In 2017, Bodie's writing returned to the big screen with the release of *I'm Not Ashamed: The Rachel Joy Scott Columbine Story*.

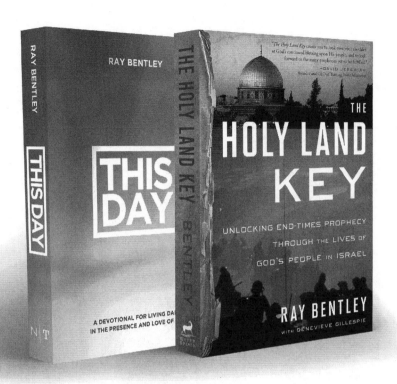

Unlock end-times prophecy with

THE HOLY LAND KEY

and learn to live daily in the presence and love of God

THIS DAY

Both are available now at
RAYBENTLEY.COM

For more books by Bodie Thoene, visit
WWW.THOENEBOOKS.COM

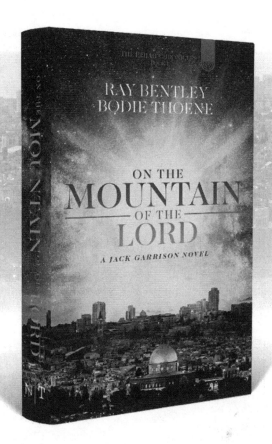

*While Jack Garrison's future
looks uncertain, the girl he loves
struggles to stay alive while
harboring a dangerous secret.*

Order book TWO of

THE ELIJAH
CHRONICLES
at RAYBENTLEY.COM

Made in the USA
Columbia, SC
01 August 2021